WHERE A GODDESS BELONGS

FORGOTTEN GODDESSES

STEPHANIE JULIAN

ONE

"Three freaking months since I was kidnapped, and I haven't had a decent drink or gotten laid the entire time. I deserve a damn medal."

Sitting on her bed in her room in a tiny cabin surrounded by a forest, Kari Vitelli, otherwise known as Akhuvitr, Etruscan Goddess of Healing, heaved a sigh and pouted.

She hadn't spoken loud enough to attract the attention of her two totally hot captors...who'd been perfect gentlemen for the past three months. And that was totally *not* cool.

Was she ugly? No, she was not. Not even by this century's wacked-out standards.

She didn't even need a mirror to tell her that. Not that her captors had allowed her to have one. She understood. She supposed if she was industrious enough, she could break it and use it as a weapon.

But that would mean she'd have to be willing to injure her two gorgeous bodyguards. And she certainly wasn't willing to do that. They were way too yummy to harm. And other than not allowing her to leave this little bungalow in the woods, they'd done nothing to hurt her.

Truth be told, when she wanted to leave, she would. No one would be able to stop her.

Well, no one who didn't want to hurt her. And she really didn't think they did.

She wasn't sure she could outrun her captors on one of their outdoor walks. And she hadn't wanted to test the locking spells on the doors and windows to see if she could break them. Didn't want to alert anyone who might be watching through the tiny cameras scattered throughout the house that she retained a pretty decent dose of her powers.

As the Goddess of Healing, Kari's powers were... Well, they weren't exactly made for blunt force, which she'd need if she wanted to leave this building on her own. Her powers were more persuasive. Much more subtle. And devastating if used in the right way. Or the wrong way, depending on your point of view.

She didn't want to use that power on her guards.

"Is it too much to ask for them to look at me and want me? Seriously, I'm not heinous."

She'd never had trouble enticing men into her bed, not in all the centuries she'd been alive. Her dark hair waved down her back to generous hips and a pretty decent ass. Her eyes were big and brown, her lips full and her nose adorable. And her tits were pretty damn near fantastic.

She had all the assets needed to be worshipped. Which she had been. For a millennium.

Lately?

Not so much.

Turning from the window with another sigh, she contemplated heading out of the bedroom and into the living room where her guards were either playing cards, watching TV or reading. She loved seeing big, brawny guys with books in their hands. Made her a little less skeptical about the direction the human race was heading.

Just a little.

Then again, Den and Jacoby weren't exactly normal humans, were they? No, they were not. But just because they were aligned with the *Malandante* didn't mean they were all bad.

Did it?

They hadn't asked to be born into the Etruscan race's equivalent of the League of Assassins, had they? And she was in no way convinced they were cut out for the roles they'd been chosen to play.

With that thought lingering in her head, Kari waved her fingers at the tiny camera in the corner of the ceiling then pushed off the bed and headed for the front room.

She didn't try to hide her approach. She'd learned she couldn't creep up on either of them. Their hearing was too good. An interesting fact she'd tucked away for later. For what purpose? She didn't know. Most likely she'd forget about it a few days after she no longer spent every waking second with these two men.

Which wouldn't be long now.

She was fairly certain she knew why she was being kept against her will. At least, she was pretty certain she knew why the *Mal* wanted her enough to kidnap a goddess.

What she didn't know was what *these* two men wanted with her. Because it damn sure wasn't what the rest of the *Mal* wanted.

"Good morning, Lady. Would you like something to eat?"

Mug in hand, Jacoby stood in the entryway to the little galley kitchen to the left of the front entrance.

Keeping a few feet between them meant she didn't have to bend her head back so far to look into his eyes. If she plastered herself against him, her cheek would rest right between his pecs. She would love to splay her hands over those pecs and stroke the tight muscles. Then she'd let her hands slide down his torso and wrap around his body to pet that tight ass.

Jacoby had the body of an athlete. Sleek. Infinitely pettable. He also had the dark eyes, black hair and strong features of a classic Roman centurian. Gorgeous.

As always, she flashed a smile at him and watched an answering warmth fill his eyes. It wasn't attraction. It was genuine warmth.

Nothing at all like the barely concealed desire she saw in Den's eyes.

But both of them were too good to let that emotion show on their faces. You could never be sure who was watching.

"Good morning, Jacoby. How did you sleep?"

"Fine, Lady. Thank you for asking. And you?"

Her smile grew. They did this dance every morning. The polite pleasantries, the offer to make her breakfast, no matter that it was close to noon.

Time to shake things up a little.

She hadn't wanted to upset the status quo until now. Hadn't wanted the men behind those cameras to think Jacoby and Den should be replaced because they were getting too close to their captive.

But since she'd overheard Den's phone conversation last night, she knew it was time. Things had changed, wheels were turning, blah, blah, blah...

Whatever, it was time to make a move.

"Actually, I would love some scrambled eggs and toast. And tea. It's a little chilly this morning, isn't it?"

Out of the corner of her eyes, she saw Den unwind his big body from the chair he'd commandeered in the living area, his attention totally focused on her. The chair was large and leather bound. And nearly too small for him.

She had images of herself riding him on that chair...while Jacoby stood to the side, his cock in her mouth.

If only.

If Jacoby was the athlete, Den was the life-sized version of an action figure. Wide shoulders, bulging arm muscles, rock-solid pecs and eight-pack abs. He hadn't touched her since the moment they'd arrived at this little cottage, wherever this may be, but she remembered in perfect detail just how strong he really was.

During her kidnapping, when he'd been accompanied by the other man—a true *Mal* down to the oily coating on his soul—he'd picked her up and carried her like she weighed no more than a child. It made her want to shiver just thinking about it.

His strong arms tight around her. The power of his legs as he ran. The solid muscles of his chest against her cheek.

It was enough to make a girl reconsider a vow of celibacy. Not that she'd taken one, of course.

Tinia's teat, how boring would that be?

Den was definitely not boring. Where Jacoby was conventionally handsome, Den...wasn't. His nose had been broken at least once and not set properly. He had beautiful, ice-blue eyes and sharp cheekbones, but the stupid women of this time probably never gave him a second look. They were probably frightened off at first glance.

Kari was *not* frightened of him. She could barely restrain herself from climbing him like her own private tree. All that yummy strength was enough to give a girl heart palpitations. Even a girl who happened to be a goddess.

Amity had always said Kari was slightly off her rocker. Kari wouldn't necessarily argue the point. Still, despite the fact that they'd kidnapped her and made it perfectly (though apologetically) clear she wasn't allowed to leave, she'd fallen completely in lust with these men. And when she left, which she planned to do in the next few days, she wanted them to come with her.

That, of course, was going to be the tricky part.

After blinking at her for a second, Jacoby finally got over his shock at her request. "Of course, Lady. Let me—"

"It's Kari, Jacoby. Please call me Kari. It's not like we haven't spent almost every second for the past three months in the same five rooms together."

His eyes narrowed slightly and she knew her slight barb had found its intended target. She figured it held a little more punch simply because it was the first time she'd even hinted at the fact that she'd been taken against her will.

"Lady Akhu—"

"If you don't mind," she turned to include Den, who'd come up behind her, "I really do prefer Kari."

Jacoby took a deep breath and his gaze shot to Den's for a split second. "Lady Kari, why don't you have a seat in front of the fire and I'll get your food ready for you."

She smiled at Jacoby and his eyes widened in response. Then she turned to Den and let her smile become just the tiniest bit warmer. And had the satisfaction of seeing him freeze.

Ah, the power of sex.

Jacoby continued to hold her on that pedestal reserved for deities—which she was, of course. But Den...

With a quirk of her lips, she slipped by Den into the living room...but not before trailing her fingertips along his wrist. Out of view of any of the cameras.

She felt him stiffen then freeze in place.

Now we're getting somewhere.

a few he hadn't known he had.

It also didn't matter that his superiors would kill him if he dared touch her. They had plans for her. Plans that didn't include their mindless muscle stripping her naked and sliding his cock as deep inside her as he could get while Jacoby watched. Or joined in. He didn't have a preference at the moment.

So either way, he was screwed. And not in a good way.

Plus, he and Jacoby had way too much riding on *their* plans. There were too many lives at stake.

But later...

Vaffanculo, he was an idiot. There was no later. He couldn't allow himself to *think* about the possibility of later.

Right now, they had to stick to the plan. Because if anyone found out what they were going to do...

Out of the corner of his eye, Den caught Jacoby making a slight motion with his hand while he said something completely different aloud. "I'll get her breakfast. Why don't you have a seat at the table, Lady Kari?"

Jacoby's hand motion wanted to know if he was okay. The great thing about knowing American Sign Language...practically no one else knew what they were saying to each other.

Den nodded and said, "Okay," answering both Jacoby's and Kari's question. To anyone watching them through the cameras, it would appear he'd responded only to Jacoby's statement.

But Jacoby understood. He knew Den better than anyone else in the world and his dark eyes made it clear Jacoby didn't totally believe him.

Didn't matter. That was the only answer his friend was getting for now.

Returning his attention to Kari, Den saw her staring at him with one golden brown eyebrow raised. As if she realized there was something going on.

Kari might have the reputation of being a hardcore party girl, but these past few months stuck in this cabin with her had shown Den that there was more to this goddess than met the eye.

But what he did see made him realize why the ancient races had willingly sacrificed themselves to their deities.

Absolutely fucking gorgeous from her brown hair that fell in waves almost to her waist to the tips of her tiny toes, nails painted with what had to be magical paint that seemed to change colors daily. Right now, it was neon blue. Yesterday it'd been a murky forest green.

When she moved to slip by him, he blinked and almost tripped over his feet in his haste to get out of her way.

He knew if she touched him, he'd do something incredibly stupid. Like wrap one of his huge hands around her tiny neck, drop his mouth over her full lips and kiss her until he couldn't breathe.

Shit.

He sucked in a sharp breath as her hair brushed against his arm as she walked to the dining table.

Fuck, he was totally losing it.

He couldn't afford to lose it. He had too much riding on his shoulders to lose his shit now.

"I'm going to walk the perimeter. Be back in ten."

He felt her gaze follow him as he moved to the door but he didn't stop. He needed a reminder of what was at stake.

Pulling out his phone, he pressed the only contact in his favorites.

"Hey Mom, how're you feeling?"

"Hello, Den. I'm fine. How are you, sweetheart?"

As always, his mother sounded thrilled to hear from him, the love in her voice evident.

But he could also tell she wasn't fine. He could hear the weakness in her voice. Weaker than the last time he'd spoken to her. When had that been? Last week? No, almost two weeks ago.

Rage boiled in his gut but he shoved it back down before it leaked into his voice. "Busy, as usual."

"I guess you still can't tell me where you are but can you at least tell me if you're eating enough? You're built like a tank. You need fuel."

This was an old argument. For years, he'd chafed under against his mom's over-protectiveness. He'd sometimes felt like he was suffocating and he'd pushed back at every opportunity.

Until he'd realized how ill she was.

"I'm eating just fine. Jacoby makes sure. You know he can't go two hours without food."

She laughed but had to stop after a few seconds to catch her breath.

A few months ago, that weakness wouldn't have been as noticeable. The disease was progressing faster than he'd expected. Which meant the time to put their plan into motion was running out.

"That boy's so skinny, he needs to eat often. Takes after the rest of his family. Especially that sister of his. That girl is a twig."

And because that was a subject he couldn't afford to get into, he steered the conversation in another direction, one sure to divert her attention.

"Have you talked to the doctor about that cough? It sounds like it's getting worse."

He could hear this mom sigh through the phone.

"No, I haven't. And I'm not going to because I know what his answer will be. Is there anything you want me to tell your dad? He's been so busy lately I'm sure he hasn't had time to call."

Which was a polite way of saying his dad still hadn't gotten over the fact that his son was considered useless among the *Mal*, only good enough to be a grunt.

"I'm sure he has been. Hate to cut this short but I gotta go, Mom. Love you."

"Love you, too, Jacoby. Stay safe, sweetheart."

He disconnected with the same warring thoughts he always had. He loved his mother enough to commit unspeakable acts. And he wanted to strangle his father for being unable or unwilling to do whatever it took to make sure his wife was healthy.

Which meant it was up to Den to make sure she was. By whatever means necessary.

His gaze turned toward the door of the cabin in a remote section of the New York Adirondacks.

Was she listening? Kari, as she insisted they call her, might act like she never took much notice of anything going on around her. But Den knew her outward indifference hid an insatiable curiosity.

Anyone watching through the security cameras only saw the flippant, totally uninterested goddess, living up to her reputation as a free spirit.

Only he and Jacoby knew how closely she watched everything, how she ate up their need. How she'd slowly been getting closer to both of them, how her fingers would sometimes brush against his skin as they passed in the hall. Or how she let her gaze stay connected to Jacoby's just a little longer than before.

Maybe—

The door opened with a creak and Jacoby stepped onto the porch. His shoulders blocked out the light from inside for a few seconds before he closed the door behind him and joined Den.

"How's your mom?"

"Getting worse, though she won't admit it."

Jacoby sighed heavily. "I'm sorry."

"Not your fault."

Jacoby shook his head and Den knew he wanted to say something else but you never knew who was listening and when. It made him want to hit something.

"You wanna go hit the bag?"

They had a small but decent workout setup in the basement, the only place in the whole house that didn't have cameras. Unless they just hadn't found them yet.

"Or do you wanna bareknuckle it out here? I'll go easy on you."

A reluctant smile curled Den lips. "You'd have to be able to land a punch first."

"It'd only take me one to knock you out."

"I'd see it coming a mile away. You telegraph."

Jacoby shrugged. "Don't need to be sneaky if you're fast enough to get out of the way."

It was an old argument and one they revisited often enough that it'd become habit. But it was still true.

"Where's the lady?"

"Sitting in front of the TV watching something on the Hallmark Channel that has the words 'prince,' 'baby' and 'bride' in the title, though I'm pretty sure they're not in that order."

"We're not supposed to leave her alone."

Jacoby's eyes rolled. "You know she's not going anywhere. We both know if she wanted to leave, she would."

Yeah, he'd figured that out already. The question was, why was she staying?

"So," Jacoby continued, "have you decided what you're going to do when this assignment's over?"

And that was Jacoby's code for "we need to talk about our plan."

The plan to steal a goddess out from under the nose of the *Malandante* while simultaneously getting his mother and Jacoby's sister away and throwing themselves on the mercy of the *lucani* king.

The plan that would probably end in abject failure but was the only one they'd come up with that had a slight possibility of working.

"No idea."

"Well, you better figure it out fast 'cause I just heard from Johnson. They're sending in another pair of guards Monday."

Holy fuck. "Did they say why?"

Jacoby shook his head. "Just got the call to let me know."

Well, shit. That meant they had three days to kidnap a goddess from the people who'd kidnapped her first.

"Maybe we should tell her what's going on."

Because Jacoby's statement skated dangerously close to speaking about their plan out loud, Den shook his head. "I don't think that's smart."

"And I'm really close to not giving a fuck." Jacoby turned back to the front door but didn't open it right away. "Sunday, Den. Gotta have our shit packed by then."

Shaking his head, Den followed Jacoby back into the cabin, where Jacoby disappeared into the basement without saying another word.

Kari stood in the opening to the kitchen, watching him intently, a slight smile on her face.

"It's such a nice night I thought maybe we could go for a walk. I'd love to stretch my legs."

Because she'd asked the same thing several times before, Den had an answer ready to go.

"I'm sorry, Lady—"

"Kari." Her smile made every muscle in his body tense. "Just Kari. Why is it so difficult for you and Jacoby to use my name?"

"Because you're a goddess."

Her laughter rang out, making every hair on his body stand on end. And made his cock harder than it already was. Now, it was stiff as a board and throbbing against the zipper of his pants, demanding he take her.

"I'm still a woman, Den. A woman with desires and needs."

Holy fuck. He could barely breathe. Was she seriously coming on to him? Could she really want him? Or was she just using him? Did she think he'd release her if she let him fuck her? What would she say if he told her exactly what he and Jacoby planned to do with her?

She took a step closer and he almost took a step back. Which was stupid. He wasn't afraid of her. The exact opposite, actually. But if he took what he wanted...

Vaffanculo, he could screw up everything.

"Den?"

His gaze sharpened on hers. What did she want?

She took another step closer and reached out to put her hand on his arm.

"What do *you* want, Den?"

Her slight emphasis on that one word hit him low in the gut. He couldn't remember the last time anyone had asked him that.

"I'm not sure I should tell you."

"You can tell me anything. I'm a really good listener."

He wanted to tell her everything. Knew, instinctively, that he could trust her.

His gaze slipped to the camera again and, in that split second, she raised her hand and cupped his jaw.

"Trust me. They can't see a thing."

His gaze locked with hers and he sucked in much-needed air. And when he released it, he released his self-imposed restraints along with it.

He did trust her. He just wasn't sure it would've mattered to him if the fucking head of the *Malandante* was behind that camera.

In a split-second, he wrapped one hand around her neck, dragged her forward and slammed his mouth down on hers. Three months of leashed desire spilled out as heat seared through him like a blowtorch flame. Her lips softened against his and every muscle in his body tightened into a steel band, every nerve ending sizzling with the contact.

His mouth devoured hers, her sweet taste exploding on his tongue and flooding him with adrenaline.

Vaffanculo, why the fuck had he waited so damn long to taste her?

He wanted to inhale her but didn't want to rush. Wanted to kiss her until she went boneless against him. His fingers itched to slide down her body, mold her curves, rub his thumb over her nipples. He'd been dying to touch her for weeks and not just the accidental, or not so accidental, brushes they'd had until now.

WHERE A GODDESS BELONGS 15

No, he wanted to shove his hands under her shirt and hold the weight of her breasts in his hands. Kari never wore a bra and the woman didn't need one. She was perfect from head to toe.

And holy fuck, the way she kissed... He didn't think he'd ever get enough. Especially not now that he'd tasted her.

And if she's only using you, hoping you'll let her leave?

Right now, he didn't give a fuck about that. He only wanted to continue to devour her. Sliding his hands down to her shoulders, he drew her closer, kissing her harder and slanting his mouth to get an even better angle. She accommodated his every move, opening her mouth to him even more.

She felt delicate under his hands, but he knew she wasn't. She wasn't one of those tiny Barbie-doll women who looked like they'd snap if you touched them. No, Kari was curved and lush and built exactly the way a woman should be.

And made for his hands, which slipped from her shoulders to her back and pressed her forward. She came willingly, her arms sliding around his waist. She wasn't tall enough to put them around his shoulders. Instead, she let her hands rest on his hips, just above the waistband of his pants. If she moved her hands under his t-shirt, she could slide her fingers beneath his pants and pet his ass.

Gods be damned, he really wanted her hands on his ass. Right now, though, he'd take what he could get.

His hands slid even lower to cup her ass. She made a soft sound low in her throat and he answered with a groan he couldn't contain. Which only seemed to make her soften more. When her tongue flicked against his lips, he let her in, let her slide inside and control the pace for several seconds before he couldn't help himself.

Need more.

With his hands on her ass, he lifted her off her feet and brought her lips on a level with his. Now her arms rose to wind around his shoulders and he chased her tongue back into her mouth. She opened to him, her lips parting so he could take her mouth more completely as her legs wrapped around his waist.

Her sleek thighs tightened and the knowledge that her pussy was so damn close to his cock nearly made his head explode. If they were naked, he'd be able to sink deep inside her right now. Just the thought made his dick throb, pressing against his zipper and demanding freedom.

He wanted to take her here and now and consequences be damned. But he had more to consider than just slaking his hunger for her.

With a sigh, he let himself kiss her for another two heartbeats before he reluctantly pulled away. The soft sound of protest she made and the way she clung to him made him want to flatten her against the nearest wall. But he had to be smart about this if he and Jacoby were going to be able to complete their plan.

He pulled away, drawing his head back far enough that she couldn't reach him. As her eyes opened, he saw no anger in expression, just curiosity. His gut clenched as another wave of lust swept through him.

Gods be damned, she is so fucking sexy.

His jaw clenched against the urge to take her mouth again but he was pretty sure if he didn't stop now, he wouldn't stop at all. He'd strip her naked and pound her against the wall until neither of them could walk.

"Why did you stop?" Her voice held lazy interest, as if she knew she could have him back where she wanted him with a snap of her fingers. Which was absolutely true.

His gaze flicked to the camera and her lips curved in one of those sweet-sexy smiles again. "Don't you trust me, Den?"

He did. But they'd spent the last three months stuck in this cabin alone with Jacoby and an ever-increasing level of lust and that was surely fucking with his head. So she'd have to excuse him if he didn't trust himself. And for all he knew, she could simply be using him to gain her release.

"I don't trust myself."

Her head cocked to the side and her expression softened. "Why is that?"

"You shouldn't trust me either."

Because he wanted—no, he needed something from her and he'd do anything to ensure his mother was safe. Her eyes narrowed and she lost the slight smile. Then she lifted one hand to his cheek and let her fingers trail along his jaw.

"What's put that look on your face?"

He thought about his response for almost a full minute. She waited quietly, her touch making him hyper-aware of her.

"We should wait for Jacoby."

Her eyebrows rose and that slight smile returned. "I'm more than happy to wait for Jacoby to return if that means I get to have you both."

His mouth dropped open before he could catch it and, as her smile widened, his gaze narrowed.

"Oh, don't look so surprised." Her laughter echoed through the room. "Don't tell me you haven't thought about it."

Shit, yeah, he'd thought about it. but it wasn't something he and Jacoby had discussed. It'd just never come up, even though they'd been friends since childhood and had the same taste in women.

Maybe it had something to do with the way they'd been brought up. Plural relationships weren't common in their circles. The *Mal* were disgustingly old-fashioned and stuck in the past when it came to relationships. Most of the men believed women belonged in the house, raising good little *Mal* babies and keeping their mouths shut while the men plotted world domination. Those men would never comprehend the fact that women were the stronger sex.

Den understood. His father hadn't but his mother had taught him how strong women had to be to put up with the shit their men did.

"Where did you go just now?"

He automatically glanced at the camera. He trusted Kari. He did. He just couldn't take the chance of someone discovering the plans he and Jacoby had made. Too many lives depended on keeping this secret. He shook his head and kept his mouth shut. Amazingly, she didn't push.

"Okay, you can keep your secrets...for now. But you know where to find me if you decide to take me up on my offer."

Then she turned and walked out into the front room. He stayed behind, trying to get his head on straight. She'd rattled him—no, not rattled. She'd cranked him up and now he wanted her more than he had before. If that were even possible.

Vaffanculo, he needed to talk to Jacoby openly. They needed to figure out how they were going to make Kari, Den's mother and Jacoby's sister disappear from three different locations at the same time.

Without getting caught or ending up dead.

Might as well wish for a miracle because that had a much better chance of actually happening.

TWO

Jacoby was only five minutes into his rounds when the woman appeared at his side.

"You look like you have the fate of the world on your shoulders. What's happened?"

He wasn't surprised by her appearance. He'd been expecting her. The only problem he had was, he still wasn't sure if she was real or if he was imagining her.

"The *Mal* are sending our replacements on Sunday. I don't think we have enough time to get everyone out before then."

"Ah, yes. That could be a problem. So what are you going to do?"

For a few seconds, Jacoby considered the fact that he was most likely talking to a figment of his imagination. She'd made her first appearance about two months ago, had scared the shit out of him as he'd made his rounds one night. He'd thought she was real...until he'd reached for her and his hand had passed right through her arm.

Freaked out and afraid he'd finally lost his mind, he tried to ignore the apparition, but she'd refused to go away. The second time she'd appeared, he'd found he could no longer ignore her and he'd asked who she was.

After she'd told him, he'd walked back to the cabin and almost confessed to Den that he was losing his mind. He'd caught himself before the words could escape and make Den worry more than he already was.

"I'm not sure. I thought we'd have more time to come up with a plan, make something work."

"Well, now you don't. Who do you sacrifice?"

Jacoby shot a glare at the female walking beside him. "No one. That's not an option."

"Sometimes it's the only option."

Stopping with a frustrated sigh, Jacoby turned to confront his imaginary friend.

She looked much more real than she had the first time he'd seen her. She held herself like a goddess and by that, he meant she looked regal. Not tall but not short, not skinny but not heavy, her hair down to her mid-back and a shade of brown that defied explanation. Somewhere between sable and gold.

And her eyes...damn, she had beautiful eyes, a brown so dark they looked almost black. They held a sharp intelligence that made him feel like an idiot every time he opened his mouth around her. Sometimes he kept it shut. This was not one of those times.

"No. Not in this case. And if you don't have anything helpful to say, I respectfully request you don't give any more advice. Unless you have something to suggest other than sacrificing someone I love."

She remained silent and, for several seconds he wondered if he'd finally stuck his foot far enough into his mouth that she'd leave and never come back. He wasn't sure that's what he wanted.

She stared at him for so long he was pretty sure she was about to blast his head off his shoulders.

And then she smiled and he swore the fucking sun shone out of her pores.

Vaffanculo, he truly was losing it.

"Good for you. I'm glad to see you're not afraid to speak your mind. You're going to need that strength."

His mouth opened as he tried to think of a response but all he could come up with was, "I don't know what the hell to do. We're screwed anyway we try to work this. And if you were really here and not just a figment of my imagination, you'd be able to help me with this problem. But since you're just part of my brain, of course you don't have anything to add because I'm well and truly screwed here."

The woman laughed, husky and low and sexy, the kind of laugh that turned men's heads and made them want her.

Except for Jacoby. He had it bad for an actual flesh-and-blood goddess who made him want to throw her down on any flat surface and lose himself in her soft body. The same goddess his best friend lusted after, as well.

Damn, we're all screwed.

"Why don't you tell me a little more about your dilemma and we'll see if we can't come up with a solution."

Sighing, he figured what the hell. "The problem is I don't know who to trust except Den. We have no allies in the *Mal*. And we don't know anyone outside of it. We're fucked." He paused. "Excuse the language."

Which just made him want to smack himself upside the head. Why the hell was he apologizing to someone who wasn't really there?

"Well, I do know someone you can trust."

Snorting, he began to walk again, not surprised when she kept pace. "Sure. Okay. Lay it on me."

"His name is Steven and I believe you may have heard of him."

He stopped short. Holy shit. She was right. Or he was right. And who the hell cared at this point. He'd never met Steven Castiglione but the guy's name was infamous among the *Mal*. Jacoby had never heard the entire story but the rumors flying among the *Mal* muscle, guys like Jacoby and Den, was that he'd defected to the *lucani* a few years ago, after he'd taken down a high-level *Mal* in Florida.

Why the hell he'd gone to the *lucani*, no one knew although there was talk of a woman being involved. Which made sense. When wasn't there a woman involved?

The woman back at the cabin immediately popped into his head. Beautiful. Sexy. And off limits.

Fuck.

"Do you know how I can get in contact with him?"

The woman put one hand on her hip and raised her eyebrows. "Oh, so you believe I'm real now?"

"Are you?"

Her laughter rang out, strong and clear and completely natural. But there was still something so...otherworldly about her.

"Who *are* you?"

Her smile softened but the look in her eyes made his back straighten. It was the look of royalty.

"Before I tell you my name, I want you to tell me something."

He nodded, his throat going dry.

"Who do you think I am?"

He hadn't been expecting that question, but he had an answer ready to go.

"Turan, Lady of the Swans."

Her smile widened slightly, enough to let him know he'd

amused her. Why? He had no idea.

If she was real, he had no idea why the Goddess Turan would be talking to him. Considering she was one of the five founding Etruscan deities who'd disappeared thousands of years ago... Even an idiot would understand his dilemma.

If she wasn't real, then, yeah, the stress was getting to him and he needed to have his head examined. But he had no idea why he would've conjured up this goddess as the voice of his conscience. It made no sense, which was why he hadn't said anything to Den or anyone. No one would've believed him anyway.

"Are you?"

He had to ask, couldn't stand not knowing.

"Are you sure you want the answer?"

No, he really wasn't but he was done screwing around. "Yes."

Her smile made all the tiny hairs on his arms stand at attention, not in fear but in awe. "And that's your answer, as well."

Shaking his head, he frowned. "How? And why me?"

"Because you called to me."

"What? How?"

She reached out to him, laid her fingers against his jaw and he realized he could feel her skin against his. His mouth dropped open in shock and he drew in an audible gasp.

What the fuck? Had he been wrong this entire time about her not being here? Had he imagined his hand going through her body like she wasn't there?

"Don't doubt yourself now, Jacoby." She drew her hand away. "I need you to be strong."

"Why?"

"Because the battle is coming."

"What battle?"

Her smile leveled out. "The battle for our return."

THREE

Kari could tell something had changed.

Jacoby had returned from making his rounds looking even more tense than he had before he'd left. He'd pulled Den into the tiny galley kitchen, where they'd held a quiet, intense conversation she hadn't been able to overhear.

Which led her to believe one of the men had a little more magic than she'd thought. Maybe more than anyone knew. Otherwise, the *Mal* wouldn't be wasting his powers guarding her. It was obvious the *Mal* thought she had very little power left or they would've set more than two guards on her. It pricked at her pride that they thought so little of her. Which was ridiculous. She should be happy they'd underestimated her. It'd make it easier for her to slip away.

The problem was, she didn't want to slip away without Den and Jacoby. She wanted them to come with her.

From her spot on the couch, where she was pretending to watch some mindless show about tiny little houses with more amenities than any mansion she'd ever been in, she wondered what had put that look on Jacoby's face. Den hadn't had time to tell him about their little scene in that same spot about an hour ago, so that couldn't be the problem.

Not that she thought it was a problem. She was hoping it would happen again, like soon and including Jacoby.

Sighing, she propped her chin in her hand and gave up any pretense of watching television. Those two were much more interesting than anyone she'd ever met before. Which was odd because she'd been around for a couple thousand years and had met millions of people in her lifetime.

So what was it about these two men?

On the surface, they were handsome, of course. But she'd met some of the most beautiful men in the world throughout her life. What set these two apart?

Den had the whole he-man protector vibe going for him, which, she had to admit, appealed to her more than it probably should in this day and age. Then again, she was a goddess so she could do as she damn well pleased. And she usually did.

Jacoby... He was still a mystery to her. Respectful to a fault but she could tell he wanted her. Or maybe she was reading something into his behavior that just wasn't there. On the outside, he seemed like the perfect *Mal* soldier, quiet and dutiful. But there was something else about him, something that made her want to dig beneath the surface and uncover all of his secrets. Because he had secrets. They shadowed the depths of those dark eyes and made her want to pull him close and pet him until he told her everything.

As the Goddess of Healing, this wasn't uncommon for her. They didn't call her Lady of the Singing Heart for shits and giggles. It was her nature to want to heal her people, to take their emotional pain and distress and leave them happier than she found them.

But what she felt for Den and Jacoby went beyond wanting to heal. She wanted so much more, something she'd never felt before. Which made her want to dig inside herself and find out why.

But first, she wanted to know what they were discussing because it certainly seemed intense.

They leaned toward each other, as if they were keeping their voices low, but Kari knew one of them was using some sort of spell to keep her from hearing their conversation. And if that wasn't interesting enough, Den was doing his fair share of the talking. He was usually the one to listen, while Jacoby talked.

It'd been almost five minutes and their conversation didn't seem to be abating. In fact, she thought it might actually be picking up speed. Jacoby was shaking his head as Den leaned back, his hands spread on the counter behind him, making his arm muscles bulge.

Damn, she really wanted him to use those arms to lift her off her feet and hold her against the wall and fuck her until she couldn't see straight. Or maybe he could hold her against Jacoby while they both took her.

Oh, the images in her head. If she wasn't careful, she'd start to drool. And how embarrassing would that be?

Pretty damn embarrassing, considering she was a freaking goddess.

Jacoby turned to look at her just then. She was sure he'd only meant to glance over and make sure she was still watching TV. But their gazes caught and held. His held a stormy indecision that made her own gaze narrow in contemplation.

He stared at her for several long seconds before he shook his head, inky dark hair falling over his forehead and his mouth flattening into a straight line, and tore his gaze away.

Slashing a hand in front of him, he responded to Den, who shook his head and said something that made Jacoby's jaw tighten even further. Whatever they were arguing about, it was intense, and they weren't in agreement. They kept going back and forth, shaking their heads in alternating turns.

Deciding she'd had enough of being left out of the conversation, she rose from the couch and made her way to the kitchen, where both men went silent and still as soon as she stood.

With a snap of her fingers, she spelled the cameras in the room to loop the last ten minutes of footage. If anyone was watching, they'd see Den and Jacoby talking in the kitchen and her watching TV on the couch.

It took more magic than she'd expended in days, and left her vulnerable in a way she didn't like to be. But she had the feeling the situation had changed and time had run out.

"Don't you think it's time to fill me in on the plan?"

The men exchanged a glance before Den straightened away from the counter where he'd been leaning and closed the distance between them. She let her head drop back so she could maintain eye contact, her lips curving in a smile she'd been told was irresistible.

Den's gaze dropped to her lips for several long seconds before he dragged it back to meet hers.

"Do you need something, Lady Kari?"

She let her smile widen and watched the heat in Den's eyes burn hotter.

"I need to know what's going on. I'm sure you know I'm not stupid—"

"No, Lady, we—"

"—and I realize that something's changed. I'd like to know what that is. I may be able to help."

They both looked at the camera in the doorway at the same time before staring at each other. Den tilted his head to the side, his eyes widening. Looking at Jacoby, she caught him shaking his head. But she didn't think he was responding to Den's silent question. He just looked frustrated.

Finally, Den said, "Things have."

"Den."

Jacoby's terse tone cut through the air like a blade but Den never broke eye contact with her.

"They're sending our replacements Monday. Which means if we're going to get you out, we have to do it soon."

"For fuck's sake, Den. You're gonna get us all killed."

Now, Den turned to Jacoby, his expression darkening. "It's now or never, Jack. We either do it or we don't. But we both know we can't *not* do something. We've run out of time."

There was an undercurrent in his voice that clued her into the fact that other pieces were in play here. She'd never been a chess player. She didn't enjoy games that didn't involve sex or wine or even ping pong balls and those cute red plastic cups filled with beer. Hell, she couldn't even finish a game of checkers without getting distracted, which usually meant flirting with her opponent and ending up in bed.

She was an unapologetically sexual creature who took emotional pain from those who needed her and sloughed off that pain with sex or alcohol. She barely ever looked beyond the pain to the resulting causes because if she did, she wouldn't be able to function. Her heart just couldn't take it. It's why she'd never settled down with any one lover for more than a couple of years. The mortals died eventually and the immortals... Well, mostly they were dicks.

These two men had piqued her curiosity and she wanted more of them. So whatever problem they were having, she needed to help them solve it. If she could.

"Tell me what's going on. I may actually be able to help."

Jacoby's scowl deepened as he shook his head but Den caught and held her gaze.

"It's not just you we need to get out. My mom and Jack's sister need to disappear, too."

The plot thickened. "Why?"

"Because my mom's sick and we know of only one person who has the same illness who was actually cured. No one else has survived." His jaw tightened and he swallowed hard before he continued. "And Jack's sister...she needs to get away before the *Mal* make her into a monster."

"Why would they do that?"

Jacoby and Den exchanged another one of those looks that expressed a whole lot more than any words could. Finally, Jacoby inhaled sharply and let it out on a sigh.

"Because they think she's your replacement."

Kari's mouth dropped open for several seconds even though she really didn't know what to say.

Her replacement?

She blinked as the world around her went a little dim. Maybe it spun, too. Reaching for the nearest flat surface to hold herself up, she instead connected with warm flesh. Jacoby had reached for her, sticking out his hand to catch her before she toppled over. Which had been a very real possibility.

My replacement.

She knew what had happened with Catene and Lucy. Lucy had been the Etruscan Goddess of the Moon until a few years ago when she'd given up her mantle of power to the young Etruscan shifter who'd been born to take her place.

I'm being replaced. What if I don't want to be replaced?

Did she even have a choice in the matter or would she simply lose her powers one day and be...just another nameless face on the street.

"Lady Kari?"

She swallowed hard, trying to keep up with her boomeranging thoughts but her brain wouldn't settle.

Would she be mortal? Would she have any magic? Would she have to get a job? What would she even do?

She didn't have a clue. She wasn't trained for anything. She couldn't do anything. She was useless—

"*Kari.* You need to breathe or you're going to pass out."

Jacoby's low, worried tone finally got through the haze of panic that had descended on her. Her gaze connected with his and she found herself a little steadier. Sucking in several long, deep breaths, she realized Jacoby had hold of her hands and was squeezing them tight. Not painfully, just tight enough for her to feel safe.

"Damn it."

Out of the corner of her eye, she saw Den run a hand through his already tousled hair, his expression angry. Not at her, at himself.

"Den."

He met her gaze, shaking his head. "I'm sorry. I'm an idiot. I shouldn't have let my fucking mouth run—"

"I glad I heard it from you and not someone else. Really." She released one of Jacoby's hands to reach for Den, grabbing the hand that was about to run through his hair again. She wanted to smooth those ruffles.

Actually, she wanted to make more of them while they were naked in a bed, but they'd deal with that situation later. Right now, she had more on her plate than she'd expected.

She needed to figure out what they were going to do because, no, she couldn't leave her successor in the hands of the *Mal.* No matter what else happened, that had to come first.

"Where is your sister?"

"New York City."

She turned to Den. "And your mother?"

"The Hamptons."

She thought about the logistics for a few seconds, thought about who she knew she could trust with this information. A few names came to mind but only one she knew wouldn't ask for anything in return and had enough leverage to actually make this all work.

"Do you have my cell phone?"

Jacoby shook his head. "Why?"

"Because I know someone who can help us pull this off, but I don't exactly have his phone number memorized."

"What's his name? Can we find him in the phone book?"

She almost laughed but then realized it wasn't a bad idea. Unless you actually knew who you were looking for, the phone book was fairly anonymous. A perfect hideout for those who didn't want the wrong people to find them.

"Actually, I think so. But we need an actual phone book. One made of paper. Find me one from Reading, Pennsylvania, and I think I'll be able to find us some help."

FOUR

"We're not sure it's authentic yet but Sal passed along a message that might have come from the men guarding Lady Kari. I may need you to go on a scouting mission."

Cole Luporeale waved Quinn Kennett into his office and motioned for him to shut the door, which he did before dropping into the chair on the other side of Cole's desk.

The *lucani* king had his head bent over a stack of papers on his desk and hadn't yet looked up. Quinn could tell his friend's attention was split in about six different ways and that made him want to smack Cole across the back of his head to get him to pay attention.

"Your wish is my command," Quinn shot back, just to see what Cole would do.

For the past few months, the *lucani* king had been...stressed. No, not stressed. He'd been more than just stressed. But he'd been hiding it well.

Quinn understood the guy was dealing with some pretty heavy shit these days. Goddesses being pursued by demons. Children being born to replace the Etruscan deities who'd served the Etruscan magical races for thousands of years. The

Mal hunting the Etruscan wolves with the intent to enslave them again.

Deep shit, all of it. And Cole believed he had to handle it all on his own.

The only thing on Quinn's mind lately was a mate who didn't want anything to do with him. Granted, Serena was more than five-hundred years old and had only just become uncursed a couple of years ago but still... He had some time on his hands, and he was Cole's second in command. He was supposed to help Cole with this shit, take some of the burden. Lately, Cole had been more close-mouthed than normal. And that scared the crap out of Quinn.

Just when Quinn thought Cole wouldn't bother to respond, the other man sighed, dropped his pencil to the desk and grimaced at Quinn.

"Damn it. Sorry. These fucking spreadsheets are giving me a fucking headache."

"What are you trying to figure out?"

Now he winced and Quinn's brows rose.

"Nothing. I mean, it's probably nothing. Hell, I'm still not sure I know what the fuck I'm looking for."

"Can I give you a hand?"

Cole pushed the papers across the desk. "Go for it."

Quinn grabbed the papers and leaned back in his chair as he scanned the first page. He immediately sat forward again. "Holy fuck. Is this what I think it is?"

"If you think it's a godsdamn recipe for disaster, then yeah, that's exactly what it is."

"Well, shit. The club's already made more money this year than it did all of last year."

Cole sighed again. "Exactly. We're supposed to run under the radar, not become a fucking hot spot."

Quinn had to laugh at the absurdity of it. "Well, it could be worse."

Cole gave a disgusted huff. "How?"

"It could get a Michelin rating."

If Quinn had hoped to get a laugh out of Cole, he'd bombed out.

"How the hell did this happen?" Cole flung a hand in the direction of the spreadsheets. "I pull you back here and things in Philly go to hell."

Well, that was a backhanded compliment, wasn't it? While Quinn had been in charge of the Philly clubs, they'd done well but not prospered like this. Which had been the point. But now his replacement was making more than Quinn had and... Yeah, it kinda sucked.

His thoughts must have shown on his face because Cole grimaced again. "*Vaffanculo.* You know I didn't— Oh, for fuck's sake."

He let Cole swing for a few seconds before he grinned, mostly unforced. "Dude, you're too easy."

Cole threw a pencil at him, which he caught just before it hit him in the face. "And you're an ass."

Quinn caught his friend's quick smile before it disappeared again under that worried grimace and his gaze dropped back to the spreadsheet. "Hey, man. You need a break. If this shit is getting to you, you need to take a step back."

"No time. Too much to do."

"I get that you're busy, but seriously, you're gonna stroke out if you don't take some downtime."

"It's not that bad."

"From where I'm sitting, it looks worse."

Cole looked up to roll his eyes at Quinn. "Don't you have enough of your own shit to worry about? How are you and Serena getting along?"

And this was why he was king. Cole knew how to shut down a conversation with one question. Because that question was just too damn hard to answer.

"We're fine."

Cole finally looked up from the desk and looked straight at Quinn. "Bullshit. You want to talk about it?"

Sure, now Cole decided to get interested in something other than those spreadsheets.

"Nothing to talk about. Serena's got her hands full and so do I."

"You know I can give you time off—"

"I don't need time off. What I need is for my king to let me do my job. You don't have to do everything yourself."

For a second, Cole looked like he might actually open up and tell Quinn what was going on. Because something was definitely going on. But after a few seconds, he just shook his head. "Fine, you want something to do? Talk to Sal, see if this information is something we need to check out. And if you think it is, go ahead and chase it down. Hell, it's the first lead we've had in months and Lady Amity's beginning to worry. And I don't need another worried goddess on my ass."

"Another?"

Cole grimaced, like he'd revealed something he shouldn't have. "It's nothing. Nothing to worry about. Cat's been...having some issues."

"Why is this the first I'm hearing about it?"

"Because she doesn't want the entire damn den knowing her business. Bad enough the girl's gotta deal with trying to figure out how to control her new powers along with all the other stuff related to growing up."

Quinn nodded in total agreement. Cat was still only a teenager but she'd taken on the mantle of the Etruscan goddess of the moon, the mother goddess of the *lucani*. She had an entire, albeit small, race of people who were looking to her to make their lives better. To have answers to questions they didn't even know they had.

"Is she okay?"

"I think so, yeah." Then he rolled his eyes. "Believe it or not I think she's having guy trouble. Only, the guy is a fucking god. Not that I blame Tivr for keeping his distance. She's only nineteen—and *vaffanculo*, I can't believe I'm talking about a godsdamn teenager and her love life."

"We're living in strange times."

"Damn right. And on top of it all, the fucking phone company wants to put a tower on den property. They'd need access for almost a month. The upside is, we'd get an upgrade on our cell and internet service."

"Yeah, but the bad side is there'd be *eteri* wandering around for who knows how long. Are you going to deny them access?"

"I don't know yet. It'll look suspicious as hell if I do and we don't need anyone getting suspicious."

"True."

Cole shook his head and sighed. "Do me a favor and check out that call from Sal."

Nodding, Quinn got up and headed for the door. "No problem. I'll let you know what I find."

"Hey, Quinn."

He stopped at the door and turned to see Cole with a half grin on his face. "Thanks."

Quinn bowed, knowing it would piss off Cole. And make him laugh, which it did.

"No problem, your royal highness."

<hr />

"I'M STILL NOT sure this was the right thing to do."

"We need to try. We're running out of time."

Jacoby shook his head, uncertainty still eating at his gut. "We're not even sure this guy's going to call back. Even with Kari vouching for us, what if he doesn't come through? What the hell are we going to do then?"

Den leaned his forearms against the porch railing, his expression resigned. "We give him until tomorrow morning. If we don't hear back, we come up with another plan."

Jacoby couldn't get to resigned. He was stuck second-guessing every move they'd made up to this point. One thing he was sure of... They should've gotten out earlier. They'd left it too late and now they were up against a ticking clock. And that was all on him. Whenever Den had wanted to plot or plan, he'd said to wait, that there'd be more than enough time to do what they needed.

But then Den's mom had taken a turn for the worse and they'd been assigned to guard Kari. And Den had fallen in lust and Jacoby... Well, he'd kept his distance. He couldn't afford to let sex get in the way of his sister's life. He had to be focused and ready for anything.

Which meant he'd already fucked up because he hadn't been ready to be pulled off Kari's protection detail. He'd thought they'd have more time. Or maybe it'd been wishful thinking.

Yeah, thinking about how you wanted to get her in your bed.

Shit. Just...shit. He needed to stop thinking about sex and start thinking about what the hell they were going to do if Plan A fell through. They'd had to be careful when they made the phone call. Kari had used her magic to trick the cameras into showing the same fifteen-minute loop but he'd been worried that someone might pick up on the fact that they appeared to be so inactive for so long. He didn't want anyone to get suspicious and send their replacements sooner.

That meant she'd had to talk fast and give only the most essential information. Where all the players were located and when their replacements would show up. Apparently, the man on the other end of the phone hadn't been all that worried about her. At least, he hadn't heard any concern in the deep voice from the other end.

Didn't she have anyone in her life who cared about her? And why the hell did that matter?

"Jack. We need to figure something out."

Jacoby looked over his shoulder at the door to the cabin. Kari was taking a shower and even though he had so much other shit on his brain, he couldn't stop thinking about her naked and wet.

"Jack?"

He dragged his gaze away from the door and met Den's. "I should warn my sister."

Den sighed and shook his head. "We talked about this. You know you can't. It has to go down this way."

"She's going to be terrified."

"But she'll be safe."

"We still don't know if the wolves will agree to help."

The plan they'd cobbled together required the wolves to snatch his sister and Den's mom practically off the street. To say it'd be practically impossible was an understatement. His sister had a personal guard at all times. Den's mother barely ever left her home and, if she did, only with her husband.

And they had to put this whole operation together in a few hours while managing to keep up the appearance that he and Den weren't planning to turn on their friends and family in the most unforgiveable way possible. Den's mother might never forgive him. But at least she had the possibility of surviving the mysterious disease that was killing her.

His sister... Emilia had been sheltered her entire life and they were about to uproot her and give her over to the people she'd been taught to view as the enemy. She was twenty-one and had never traveled more than a few miles from her home.

He and Den would never be safe to be around. The *Mal* would hunt them relentlessly.

"Jack." Den's blade-sharp tone cut through the fog in his brain. "Control it, man. You're about to blow."

Holy shit.

His gaze dropped to his hands, clenched into fists on top of the railing. The wood below was scorched. A few more minutes and he might've set the whole damn porch on fire. With a power no one but Den knew he had.

"I need to walk it off."

Den's hand clamped on his shoulder before he could walk away. "Don't go far."

The unease he saw in Den's eyes made Jacoby's guilt increase. Den had enough worry about. He didn't need to add to the weight on his friend's shoulders.

Nodding, he stepped off the porch and started to walk.

———

DEN WATCHED Jacoby stalk off into the woods surrounding the cabin. He could sense his friend's raging uncertainties but had no idea how to ease them because he was dealing with the same. But they couldn't stop now. The plan they'd set in motion needed to progress if they had any hope of getting his mom and Jacoby's sister out.

And keeping Kari safe.

"What's wrong with Jacoby? He's upset."

Turning, he saw Kari standing in the doorway to the cabin, her gaze following Jacoby as he disappeared into the trees.

"Nothing. He's fine. How are you, Lady Kari?"

Her smile made his cock harden. How the fuck was he

supposed to keep his head in the game when all he wanted to do was strip her naked and pound her against the nearest flat surface?

He supposed he should be respectful. She was a goddess, after all. But he only saw the woman, which would probably be his downfall. The ancient myths and legends were filled with stories of men who foolishly thought they could screw around with the gods and get out alive.

He should probably take that into consideration the next time he thought about putting his hands on her.

"I'm fine, thank you. I just needed a little fresh air. It's gotten so much colder just in the last few days. I'd love to have a fire tonight."

"Of course." Den bowed his head. "Anything you'd like."

"Well, now, that's a leading statement, isn't it?"

Shit. He really needed to watch his mouth. The *Mal* could still send their replacements tomorrow and that would fuck up everything they were trying to accomplish. But he hadn't been able to get this morning's kiss off his mind. The memory popped into his head at least every five minutes and was getting harder and harder to ignore.

He should've told Jacoby, should've come clean but... Jacoby had way too much on his mind already. Den just needed to hold it together for a few more days. Then he could let her burn him to ash if that's what she wanted.

After she and his mother and Jacoby's sister were out.

"I'm sorry, Den, I didn't mean to make you uncomfortable."

"You didn't. At least, not in a way I don't enjoy."

And there was that smile again. The one that made him want to say "fuck it" to everything, drop to his knees and worship her with his mouth right here on the porch. Jacoby would probably have a seizure when he got back. Then again, maybe it would be the push he needed to admit he had the same feelings for this woman, this goddess who appeared to want him as much as he wanted her.

Den would have no problem sharing her with his best friend. He'd be happy to have any part of her at all. He knew it wouldn't last, that he'd only be a temporary plaything for her. He'd be good with that.

"Why don't you come back inside? I'll help you build that fire. We can talk."

His gaze narrowed. "Talk about what?"

Usually when people wanted to talk, it was bad news.

She shrugged. "I'd just like to know more about you."

Pushing away from the porch railing where he'd been leaning, he waved her ahead of him into the cabin and headed for the rustic stone fireplace in the center of the room.

"There's not much to tell. I'm a soldier. When I graduated from high school, I went straight into training. When I finished after two years, I got my assignment and I've been living here in New York ever since."

"Do you like working for the *Mal*?"

He set up the fire and put a match to the paper beneath the logs before he answered. Gave him time to think about his answer.

"It's all I've ever known. The first four years, I worked building security until someone higher up realized I had a few more brains than the average grunt."

Curling herself into the corner of the couch in front of the fireplace, she patted the cushion next to her. He really wanted to take it. He also didn't want to test his restraint. So he left that seat open and took the one on the other end. It left a couple of feet between them and did nothing to help his restraint. Not when she looked so damn sexy. Before he'd met her, he'd thought sexy meant anorexic women in expensive underwear.

Now...

She wore a long-sleeved, v-neck t-shirt that clung to her full breasts and made it clear she wasn't wearing a bra. Her skirt was loose and fringed and hid her legs to just above her ankles but still showed off her curved hips. He couldn't think of any woman who would tempt him more right now. Especially with that smile that made it clear she knew what he was doing and exactly what he was thinking.

"You're not just muscle, though, are you?"

Tricky question. And one he couldn't answer honestly. There were some things he couldn't even trust to tell her.

"I'm a soldier."

Her smile tilted in a way that told him she understood what he wasn't saying.

"So how long have you and Jacoby known each other?"

The question threw him for a second. "Since grade school."

"Private, I assume. The *Mal* don't sent their children to just any school, do they?"

"I thought you said you didn't know much about the *Mal*?"

"That makes me a bad goddess, doesn't it? We're supposed to love all our subjects. You have to admit, some are easier to love than others, though."

Especially those who worshipped you and didn't kidnap you so they could force you to give your powers to your successor.

And this was a conversation they probably shouldn't be having now.

"Would you like to watch TV, Lady?"

Again, her smile made his gut hollow and his cock jerk in his pants.

Fuck.

"I'm good just watching the fire for now, but thank you, Den."

And he was fine sitting here watching her. Waiting for a call that let him know their plan was a go.

────────────

KARI FORCED herself to keep her gaze on the fire instead of staring longingly at Den. If anyone was watching, they'd surely see the hunger in her eyes and that could lead to questions and questions could lead to the *Mal* thinking maybe they needed to get new guards in place immediately. And nothing had been set in motion yet for the rescue of Den and Jacoby's family.

Even though she had no plans to stay here without these two men, she didn't want anything to happen to their loved ones. Especially not if she somehow caused them harm.

So she sat quietly, watched the flames dance and hoped Sal came through. It would take time to set up a plan, but she had faith that Sal could do it. The *salbinelli* had hundreds of years of experience as a master gamesman. If the CIA ever enticed him to work for them, the United States would know every secret of every world leader. He was just that good. The timing of everything was the problem.

Sighing, she realized she'd just have to wait for things to play out. Though she really wasn't a patient person. Den, on the other hand, seemed perfectly at home with stillness. Jacoby was more like her, though he had way more control. Like now. She wanted to jump Den's bones, let him strip her naked on the couch so she could ride him right in front of the fire.

Another sigh, this time louder and more heartfelt.

Tinia's teat, she was horny.

The sound of footsteps on the front porch made her turn toward the door as her heart began to beat just a little harder. And when Jacoby pushed open the door and walked through, she had to suck in air.

Had she really been so deprived in the past few years that she was practically panting over these men? Or was there just something different about them?

He strode straight for the couch, for them, his gaze flipping to the camera in the corner for a millisecond before flashing at her then locking with Den's.

"Tomorrow night."

She didn't understand what he was saying right away but Den sat forward, as if he was going to stand, then thought better of it. He nodded instead and watched Jacoby walk around to the fireplace and thrust his hands out toward the heat.

"The *lucani* will take care of the rest."

She had trouble hearing him because of the way he was standing, and she realized that was deliberate. His voice was pitched just low enough that it wouldn't be picked up by the cameras.

"Seriously?" Den sounded shocked. "Do you think we can trust them?"

Jacoby's shoulders lifted and fell. "Doesn't matter at this point. It's out of our hands."

Den's big body tensed, and all his nervous energy transmitted to her in waves of anxiety.

She couldn't ignore it. She reached for his hand, clenched into a fist on his thigh, sliding her fingers around his and releasing her powers to do what she'd been created to do. The force of his fear hit her like a punch to the gut and she sucked in a sharp gasp. Closing her eyes, she opened herself to it and let it in, let it fill her with its toxic power as it drained from Den.

She vaguely heard Den mutter, "What the fuck," before he attempted to draw away his hand. She tightened her hold on him, keeping his hand in place.

"Kari, what—"

"Quiet." Her voice held a command she barely ever used anymore. Never really had to. Most people who came to her for aid or who she helped without their knowledge were happy to have a respite from the emotional pain they lived with on a constant basis.

Den fell silent but he wanted to resist her. That wasn't acceptable.

Lifting her chin, she looked into his eyes, smiling when he didn't look away.

"Let me in." Her thumb stroked over the back of his hand, the warmth of his skin seeping into her own. "This is who I am. It's what I do. Let me help."

"Den?"

The sharpness of Jacoby's tone didn't distract her, she kept her focus squarely where it was needed at the moment. She'd deal with Jacoby in a few seconds.

"Just let go, Den. You don't need to carry all that weight."

He was carrying so much anxiety, so much of it buried for so long, it nearly overwhelmed her. Or maybe she was just out of practice. It'd been a few years since she'd come up against anyone with walls as thick as Den's. Most of the people she helped had reached a point where they were so desperate for any kind of help, they let her in immediately. She didn't have to fight them for access.

Den wasn't fighting but he wasn't giving in either. She supposed that's what made him such a strong soldier. Jacoby would probably be the same. Would they understand that if she helped ease their anxiety they'd be able to think more clearly? Or would they see her interference as meddling?

Pushing ahead, she maintained eye contact, searching for an opening, poking and prodding until she found a way in. And realized it was only because he allowed her in. The thought filled her with joy and she pushed that emotion through that opening, watching Den as some of the darkness lifted from his expression.

He allowed her connection to continue for several long seconds as she took some of his mental burden and replaced it with something lighter, sunnier. She felt herself sinking deeper, felt the darkness taking over but she could tell he wasn't completely healed.

"Kari."

She felt him start to pull away and gripped him even tighter.

"Lady Kari, let him go."

Jacoby grabbed her shoulders and pulled her back as Den finally tugged his hand away from hers with an audible gasp.

"Jack, catch her."

She had no idea what they were talking about. She only knew she hadn't finished and she needed to finish what she'd started. The well inside her hadn't been filled and it wanted more. That secret well she never told anyone about, not even her sister, though she suspected Amity knew it was there. That dark well wanted more.

As she closed her eyes, Jacoby pulled her away from Den and folded his arms around her to draw her into his body. His rock-solid chest pressed against her back and now she was hit with a whole other set of sensations. Jacoby held a pit of sadness that exceeded Den's anxiety. And that dark well leaped for it eagerly.

Letting her head fall back against Jacoby's shoulder, she turned and put her lips against the bare skin of his neck. He shuddered at the contact, lust roaring up along with the sorrow, making her power giddy with anticipation.

"Oh, fuck."

Jacoby's low curse fired her lust to an even greater degree, making that low burn in her gut spread throughout her body.

Without thought, she turned into Jacoby's warm strength, her mouth seeking his.

"Kari, wait."

She didn't want to wait. She wanted what she wanted and she wanted it now. She'd waited long enough. Rising onto her knees, she wrapped her arms around Jacoby's neck and unerringly found his mouth with hers. He froze, his lips still beneath hers...but he didn't push her away. His arms tightened just enough for her to know he wasn't immune.

So good to know she hadn't lost her touch. Now to make him—no, make *them* give her exactly what she wanted.

Sex. Adoration. Warmth. Comfort.

Sweaty, steamy pleasure. Hot, athletic sex.

These two men would be more than up to the task. And she wasn't about to take no for an answer. They'd have to be gone by tomorrow afternoon at the latest, anyway. Who cared what anyone behind those cameras saw? It only added to the pleasure anyway.

Rising onto her knees, she straddled Jacoby's thighs and stared into his startled eyes. Yes, she saw resistance there, but she also saw desire and that's what she focused on. She brought it to the surface and then fed her own into it. She saw the second it hit him, her lips curving into a smile as he gave himself over to it.

And when he leaned in to kiss her, she met him halfway.

Their lips meshed in a rush of heat, his hand coming up to hold the back of her head steady for his all-out erotic assault. It was her turn to moan as he opened his mouth over hers and kissed her like he wanted to inhale her. His tongue immediately invaded when she opened to him, sliding against her tongue with only one intent. He wanted to drag her down into that burning hot pit of lust with him.

She had no problem following him down.

Her hands wrapped around his neck as she turned her head, determined to give him more and better access. He kissed like he'd taken a master class in the subject and she found herself on the receiving end of unrequited lust.

It hit her like a category-five hurricane, threatened to drown her. Every nerve ending in her body lit up and began to yearn for more. She didn't plan to deny herself.

Moving her hands into Jacoby's hair, she tugged on the short strands, causing him to kiss her even harder. His hands, which he'd kept securely on her shoulders, crept down her arms. His tight hold made her want to struggle just so he'd have to grip her even tighter. She'd never been averse to a few ropes or even a paddle. Sometimes a little pain was a good thing.

Right now, though, she felt nothing but pleasure.

As Jacoby's hands continued their way down her arms, she moved closer, pressing her breasts against the firm wall of his chest. The heat pouring off him made her want to strip down to bare skin so she could feel it all over.

She breathed in through her nose, not wanting to break contact with his mouth. All she could smell was him. Male spice and something deeper, darker.

When his hands reached her hips, he yanked her closer. The move left her gasping and so turned on she thought she might actually come if he put his hands anywhere near her clit. She was so close to coming just from his kiss that she was beginning to feel a little embarrassed. And she was never embarrassed, especially not by sex. It was the most natural thing in the world. Nothing to hide and definitely worthy of being celebrated.

But right now, she wanted him to give her what she needed.

Without hesitation, she grabbed the hem of her shirt and tugged it up, breaking their kiss only long enough to get the shirt over her head then leaning forward again to crush their lips together.

She tasted his surprise in his sudden hesitation, but he got back with the program fast enough. His hands slid up from her waist to her ribs, pausing there as if asking permission. She gave it by leaning even closer. He took the hint and covered her breasts with his hands.

Moaning into his mouth, she arched until he cupped her breasts completely and squeeze.

Yes, that's what she wanted. What she needed.

More.

He took the hint and squeezed harder, pinching her nipple between his thumb and forefinger and sending a blast of sharp pleasure through her body. When she gasped into his mouth, he stilled until she thrust her breasts even more fully into his hands.

That finally seemed to cut through the last of his resistance. One hand slid behind her back and pulled her even closer while the hand on her breast tightened.

Tinia's teat, she hadn't realized how starved for affection she'd been. How much she'd needed this contact. But she knew just anyone wouldn't have satisfied her.

There was something about these two men...

And no, she hadn't forgotten about the other man. She knew Den was still at her back. She felt his gaze like a physical caress, watching her and Jacoby. She sensed that he was biding his time, not feeling ignored. He was waiting for an opening. Probably because he knew Jacoby needed a little more convincing.

So she'd be sure she had Jacoby fully on board before moving forward. That would be no hardship. Especially not while Jacoby teased her nipples into tight points that were begging for his mouth. They ached, tight and hard, and, if he didn't move his mouth there soon, she would—

Jacoby pulled back, leaving her gasping in surprise, which turned into moan when he strung a line of stinging kisses from her chin to her jaw and down her neck. He added a couple of bites that made her shiver, which made him bite harder. She'd have marks. And she'd smile every time she saw them.

Tilting her head to give him more access, she felt the hand he had on her back wrap around her hair and tug. Sensation sizzled along her scalp, zinging to her nipples and down to her clit, already needy and tight. She needed him to put a hand between her legs and relieve that needy ache. Wanted to put her hands on hard male flesh and rake her nails down his naked back while he pounded into her.

Actually, she wanted two sets of hands on her body. Yes, she was greedy. And so very, very horny. As Jacoby continued kissing his way down her body, she turned her head to look over her shoulder at Den.

She wasn't surprised to see him watching them. But the inferno of heat in those ice-blue eyes made that ache between her legs intensify. She moaned unintentionally, surprised by the need in the sound.

Jacoby pulled away a second later, his breathing labored, and she tightened her hold on him, silently urging him to continue what he'd been doing.

She wanted more. Needed more. She no longer cared who was watching. Frankly, she hadn't before but she'd been conscious of the fact that Den and Jacoby had been.

But now... She wanted everything they had to give.

"We're at your service, Lady." Den's voice made her stomach tighten into a solid ball while her blood flowed like lava through her veins. "Whatever you want.

Had he read her mind? Her lips curved in a smile that made that dark light in Den's eyes shine even brighter.

And that dark well of power she constantly battled for

control receded slightly under the onslaught of Jacoby's kisses and the obvious lust in Den's voice.

"We're here to serve you."

Service. No, that's not what she wanted. She didn't want adoration either. She wanted what she'd been missing all these long centuries, what she'd yearned for and had never found. She wanted what her sister had found. She wanted to be loved for who she was, not what she was or what she could do.

That realization threw her out of the moment. Blinking, she drew in a quick breath. Den's gaze narrowed and she could tell he'd realized something had changed.

"Kari?"

Jacoby retreated another few inches, pulling away from her hold, and she felt his gaze on her now, watching her intently. She looked between the men, looking for something she knew she wasn't going to find.

"Are you okay?"

She nodded quickly. "Yes, I'm fine. I'm sorry, I just—" Want more than you can give. "I'm not sure now's the time to start this."

Tinia's teat, that was a lame excuse. And a complete lie. Now was the perfect time. If they were going to disappear, they'd need her at full strength. And nothing recharged her batteries more than sex.

So why the hell are you turning down freely offered sex?

Damn good question.

Den and Jacoby exchanged a glance and Jacoby released her a second later. She immediately missed the warmth of his hands on her body and wanted to smack herself silly.

"You're right." Jacoby sounded remorseful but not at all angry. "I'm sorry—"

"Oh, no. Please don't be sorry. I'm really hoping we can do this again...somewhere more private."

She smiled at both men to make sure they understood she meant to include both of them and was relieved when they both smiled back, though Jacoby still looked unsure.

"We want that, too, Lady Kari. But for now, I think we need to get the hell out of here."

She didn't disagree with Den. She simply hated being denied what she wanted. And she wanted these men.

"Then I guess we should be on our way."

"I'll start packing." Jacoby headed toward the bedrooms at a pace that should've made her head spin. Damn. He practically ran away from her. That was a serious blow to the ego, wasn't it?

And you really need to get over yourself a little more.

Turning back to Den, she found him watching Jacoby with frustration plainly visible on his face.

Well, at least she wasn't the only one.

His gaze snapped back to hers when he realized she was staring at him and gifted her with a lopsided smile.

"Lady—"

"Please don't call me that, Den. My name is Kari. I'd really like you to use it."

And now she was being a total bitch. But when they called her "Lady," they reminded her that they thought of her as something "other." Something apart. She didn't want to be separate. She wanted to be a woman, not a goddess. At least to these two men. And in a few months, she'd probably be bitching about the fact that she was going to be replaced.

Damn it.

Den's head kicked to the side for a few seconds before he nodded, which looked almost like a bow, which made her want to roll her eyes.

Ugh, she had to stop this shit. Seriously.

"Whatever you want...Kari."

Oh. Wow.

Her heart skipped a beat at the renewed heat in his eyes. And she wanted to squeeze her legs together to ease the ache between them. They so needed to get far away from here so she could indulge herself in them for an uninterrupted stretch of time. Like, say, a few days.

"Is there anything you want me to pack for you? Anything you want to take with you?"

"No. If you recall, I only had the clothes on my back when we left."

"Then why don't you wait for Jack and me in the living room? We'll be ready to go in a few minutes."

"Can I help?"

He shook his head. "We just need to get our weapons. Neither of us brought anything with us we'd miss if we leave it behind. The only thing I need is to know my mom will be safe. Everything else is just stuff."

Oh. This man had a heart a mile wide, something she was sure the *Mal* had tried to beat out of him. And yet, he'd managed to maintain it. His strength drew her like a moth to a flame.

If you're not careful, you'll get your wings singed.

And then there was Jacoby, who held the weight of the world on his shoulders and hid the stress from the world. That man had hidden so much, had dark places in his soul that called to her, but he wouldn't let her in. She wasn't sure he ever would.

With a bright smile to send Den off to get ready for their departure, she wandered back to the living area and sat on the couch, quietly and out of the way. Which made her feel twice as useless as normal.

Her nose wrinkled. She really needed to shake off this pitiful-me attitude. It wasn't doing anyone any good. So, what could she do to help them get ready to leave?

She really didn't have anything here she wanted to take

with her. They'd kidnapped her with literally only the clothes on her back and these just happened to be the same clothes. They'd provided her with others but she this was her favorite skirt. Good thing she'd decided to wear it today. Or maybe her sister, Nortia, Goddess of Fate, had given her a mental clue that she should choose to wear it today.

It was true that fate could be a bitch. But it was also true that family stuck together. Mostly.

When she heard the slight noise from outside, she had to wonder if that, too, was Nortia, alerting her to the fact that someone was approaching.

She turned to look out the front window and saw nothing out of the ordinary. Just the same trees that had always been there. But were there a few extra shadows lurking?

Yes, she was pretty sure there were. And they were moving. The air was not. Guess their time had run out sooner than they'd expected. Obviously someone had been monitoring their discussion and must have sent someone earlier today. Unless they had someone like Sal who could use magic to send people elsewhere. She'd thought there was only one of Sal remaining. Truly the last of his kind. Or was he?

What other secrets could the *Mal* be hiding? Probably more than she wanted to know.

Since she didn't want to risk calling out to Den and Jacoby, she got up off the couch and headed for the kitchen, getting a glass out of the cupboard and going to the faucet in front of the window.

As she filled a glass with water, she checked out the shadows in the backyard. Yep, definitely a few out here, too. If she opened herself up to the emotion of the others outside, she could probably figure out how many they were dealing with but she was still a little raw from dealing with Jacoby's emotions. Too much and she could overload and would be no good to them when they needed to leave.

Then again, they probably should know what they were up against. And why they weren't moving in already.

What were they waiting for?

At this point, it probably didn't matter. She had faith that Jacoby and Den would do what they could to get her out of here. And she wouldn't let anyone harm them. The *Mal* really hadn't done their homework on her—

Someone grabbed her arm and she almost shrieked like a little girl before she realized it was Jacoby, standing just out of sight of anyone on the other side of the window. He held one finger to his mouth and motioned her back.

As nonchalantly as she could, she turned from the window and walked toward Jacoby. That's when she felt it. A presence she couldn't mistake. Her stomach clenched in on itself and her skin crawled. An intense sensation of dread threatened to steal her ability to breathe.

She barely felt Jacoby grab both her elbows to steady her as she swayed on her feet, every one of her senses attuned to the evil somewhere outside the cabin.

"Kari, what's wrong?"

He didn't sound worried but that quickly changed when she didn't respond. She couldn't respond. Fear held her hostage.

"Kari?"

Jacoby accompanied his sharper tone with a shake that managed to break through the black fog that seemed to surround her.

Blinking, she met his gaze. As she watched his eyes narrow, she knew she must look as if she'd seen a ghost. Or more precisely, a demon.

"What's wrong?"

He kept his voice so low she almost couldn't hear him, and it took her several seconds before she could speak. Her throat burned like she'd swallowed acid and her heart pounded so hard, she wasn't sure it didn't hurt.

"Kari? Christ, what—"

"There's something out there."

She could barely hear her own voice, but she definitely heard her fear. And so did Jacoby.

Grabbing her arm, he dragged her behind him. Even through the black pit of terror eating away at her guts, she recognized the change in him.

He'd gone from man to soldier in the blink of an eye. She'd never seen this side of him and she watched in awe as he reached above his head and ripped out the cords to the camera. Then he herded her out of the kitchen and back into the living area. Den stepped out the bedroom a second later, gun in his hand, his expression set in the same lines as Jacoby's.

Focused and intent. No one would ever mistake them for anything but soldiers right now. With Jacoby's hand on her arm urging her to keep moving, Kari forced herself not to freak. But it was hard to do when an actual demon from Aitás, otherwise known as the Etruscan version of hell, showed up at your door.

Her sister goddesses had faced them and lived to tell the tale. She would, too. Shaking off a bit of the fear, she kept her feet moving in the direction Jacoby was pointing her. Straight to Den.

"Stay behind me." Den not only had a gun in hand but another one stuck in the back of his pants and a knife on his belt. "If I tell you to run, don't hesitate and don't stop. Call the *lucani* when you can. Make sure they've got Jacoby's sister and my mom. Make sure they hold up their end of the bargain."

"You can do that yourself when we get out of this."

Den's quirky little grin eased a tiny bit more of that fear. "I have no plans of not finishing what we started, Kari. I just need to know you've got our backs."

Nodding, she got a true smile from Den.

"Then we're good." His smile disappeared. "If you get the chance, run. We'll keep them off you as long as we can."

She nodded, though she knew she wouldn't leave them. They wouldn't be able to handle the demon without her, and she refused to run while they risked their lives for her.

"Jacoby's got your back." Den ran his hand over his gun and it made a metallic *snick* that made her shudder. "Don't leave yourself open to attack. Do whatever you have to to get away. And don't stop once you start running. Jack?"

"Yeah."

Another gun cocked, this time at her back. She really hated that sound. It was so cold and so...brutal.

Of course, magic was just as deadly and infinitely more terrifying. Her own magic could be vicious if used the wrong way. That was a secret she'd prefer not to share but if she had to use it to save these two men against a demon, she would. All bets would be off.

"We've got a car stashed a few miles away." Den spoke to her in an almost inaudible whisper, moonlight streaming through the windows and highlighting the lines of his face. "Due south. If we get separated, head that way. If you reach the car before we do, take it and don't wait. Jack and I are fully capable of finding our own way. The key's hidden under the mat in the backseat."

His gaze flipped to Jacoby for a second before settling back on hers. "Don't get caught."

His rough demand made her smile. "Same goes for both of you."

He nodded then looked at Jacoby. "Five plus whatever the fuck that creepy thing is. I'd say incapacitate, but we both know we can't come back. Butch and Sundance, man. Wasn't that your fantasy?"

"Hell, I haven't seen that movie in years." Jacoby scoffed and she heard amusement in his voice. "Besides I can't swim, you know that."

They were making jokes. Shaking her head, she couldn't believe they were so calm in the face of danger that made a goddess shiver. Then again, maybe it was better they didn't know exactly what they were up against. She certainly had enough fear for the three of them. Because she knew what a demon like the one that was out there could do to them.

"I know this seems like it should be obvious, but don't let it bite or scratch you," she said. "Their venom is a paralytic and you'll be defenseless."

Both men nodded then Den headed for the bathroom. She had a second to wonder why then realized the small window would be just big enough to Den to get through, meaning she and Jacoby would have no problem. If there was no one waiting there for them.

The window slid open without a sound, as if someone had made sure it wouldn't. She was pretty certain that was no coincidence. These men had tried to take every move into account.

Now they needed a little luck.

Which they seemed to get. Den made it out the window, silent as a cat. There was no way she would be as graceful or as quiet. And if she used her magic, the demon might get a whiff of it and pinpoint their location, so that was out.

As she climbed out, Den grabbed her around the waist and lowered her to the ground, where the leaves crunching beneath her feet sounded like an explosion.

She would've stayed frozen in place if Den hadn't motioned for her to follow him as Jacoby followed noiselessly behind.

They headed for the trees surrounding the cabin, no sign of

a path in sight and the footing unsteady. She had to focus intently to stay on her feet because of the uneven ground. The cute little sneakers she'd found in her closet hadn't been made for this kind of terrain and didn't provide a lot of protection but there was no way in hell she was going to mention that.

If she had to, she'd walk out barefoot and grateful. And when Den said run, she'd run.

They were at least five-hundred yards from the cabin when she heard the sound of crashing footsteps from behind them. Just before Den grabbed her hand and started to haul ass.

She had a second to suck in a deep breath and then all she could concentrate on was making sure she didn't fall or trip. She didn't want to slow them down. She could tell Den was holding himself back for her, which meant she had to go faster for him. It sucked that she was the one holding them back. It really sucked that she was actually getting winded.

Damn it, she was a goddess. She shouldn't be out of breath. Just added insult to injury when you considered that she was fairly obsolete to begin with. Yet the only reason these men were now in danger was because they wanted her to pass on her powers to her replacement.

Her toe caught an edge and she stumbled for several steps. Den's tight hold on her hand kept her upright.

Her skin crawled as the most overwhelming wave of fear hit her. Now she did go down. She tripped over her feet and went to her knees, teeth clenching with the force of the impact. The air rushed out of her, leaving her gasping and in shock. But she had no time to take stock. Den literally yanked her back to her feet and pulled her along.

When the first shot rang out, she couldn't tell which way it'd come from. She only knew it was close. A sound that was pretty damn close to a squeal left her mouth but she was too terrified to be embarrassed. And too out of breath. But when she wasn't so damn scared anymore, someone would pay for that, damn it. Because on the heels of the fear, she was fast getting pissed.

She was a goddess, an actual living deity who deserved a hell of a lot better treatment than she was getting at the moment. If someone dared hurt Den or Jacoby, there would be hell to pay. Seriously, she was going to do damage.

And, gods damn them to Aitás and back, but she was just about ready to stand her ground and consequences be damned. Because she was already sick and tired of running.

She had power, power she'd been hoarding and hiding for years, power she'd been afraid of simply because she knew she was an aberration among her sisters. While their powers had diminished, hers had stayed at the same level.

She had an idea why but now wasn't the time to even think about that.

Now was the time to act. But she couldn't focus while she was running for her life. She was really tired of running.

But first, she needed to break Den's hold, which wouldn't be easy. He was trying not to hurt her but he wasn't going to let her go. She hated to do it but she needed to use her power on him to make him let her go. Neither man was going to like it but it couldn't be helped. It only took a few seconds for her to gather the tiny bit of power she needed to make Den release her. It hurt her heart to make him fear her, even for those few seconds.

She felt the shudder run through his arm just before he let her go. He faltered, putting a few steps between them before he stopped. Jacoby almost ran into her back but, at the last moment, pulled up and took a step to the side so he didn't touch her.

"What the fuck?"

"Kari—"

"Stand back. Don't get close."

"Fuck that." Den's voice held a distinctive growl. "Whatever you're planning to do, it's not happening."

Though she appreciated their concern and accepted that she did need protection, now was probably the time to clear up any misconceptions about needing to be managed.

She heard their pursuers getting closer with every second and knew they'd be here soon. It was now or never.

"Step back, both of you."

She caught a glimpse of the surprise on both men's faces and gave herself a tiny pat on the back. She hadn't had to use that tone of voice for years. Decades. Good to know she could still bring a little shock and awe to the proceedings. Even if she was fighting to keep her own fear from dragging her down. She couldn't let it get the best of her now. Not if she was going to be of any use to them.

Neither man had moved, though, and the demon and men chasing them had almost caught up. Too late to stop. She only hoped she could shield Den and Jacoby enough for them to be functional after this, at least enough to run.

A second later, the demon stepped into view and nearly derailed her entire plan.

There was a reason these creatures had been condemned to hell. They were scary as fuck from their inky black hair and blue skin to their fangs and claws. Even scarier, this one was dressed in human clothes. A perfectly pressed three-piece with a white shirt and silk tie.

Tinia's teat, now she wanted to run screaming in the other direction. Did it honestly think anyone would ever mistake it for human? Maybe it just didn't care? And who the hell would even think to buy this thing a suit?

Then it smiled. She wanted to wash her eyes with bleach and scrub her exposed skin raw. She wondered how the *Mal* could stand to be within five miles of it much less five feet.

"Hello, Akhuvitr. So nice to meet you."

The fact that it spoke ancient Etruscan wasn't lost on her. It had done that deliberately, to throw her off. There were very few people who still spoke the old language, very few who still understood it.

Damn it, she was *not* going to let this thing get the upper hand on her.

Standing tall, or at least as tall as she could, she stared back into those soulless black pits they called eyes and refused to flinch.

"Demon, I command you back to hell. You have no place in this world."

It smiled, and she had to stiffen every muscle in her body so she didn't cringe. And when her stomach threatened to revolt, she swallowed and, through sheer force of will, didn't puke. Though she really, *really* wanted to.

"Ah, but that's where you're wrong, Lady Kari. That's what you prefer to be called now, isn't it? Lady Kari. Has a nice modern ring to it. I like it."

"You don't belong here, demon. I command you to return."

Showing its pointed teeth again in a hideous approximation of a smile, the damn thing shrugged. As if it didn't have a thing to be worried about. And when five men materialized out of the woods to flank it, she wondered if maybe it was right.

At least one of those five men was a full *Mal*. She felt his power rub up against hers. But where hers was undiluted, his was dark and oily. That's the only way she could describe it.

Her power came from a pure well, from the same source as her brothers' and sisters' powers, drawn from the earth and the air. The demon's powers came from an offshoot of that well, a dark place that fed them what they needed to survive in Aitás.

"I could argue the same of you, Lady. Your time came and went about a thousand years ago. You're obsolete."

Asshole prick. "And your time will never come."

"I could argue that you're wrong, but I think you already know that. I'm more at home in this day and age than you will ever be. Don't you think it's time to throw in the towel? Your powers are practically nonexistent. You don't need them anymore. Aren't you tired of being so damn useless?"

She'd never admit that the thing had a point. But it did. Then again, it only had a place here because someone had invited it. The *Mal* had invited it. And that was unacceptable.

"You're wrong." She wanted to add "asshole" to that sentence but decided to take the high road. "Compassion is never useless. It's the best defense against evil."

The demon laughed and gooseflesh sprang up on her arms. "That's such a quaint way of looking at things. And also, the wrong way. It's probably going to get you killed."

Well, he wasn't wrong there, either. "But it won't be by your hand, asshole."

High road be damned. She'd had enough banter. She wanted to kill the thing or at least banish it back to Aitás. She wasn't sure she had enough power to do that but she did have enough to do this.

Drawing up power in a rush so fast, she knew she'd be paying for it for hours, she raised her hand and directed it out. The tiny amount of fear she'd instilled in Den and Jacoby to get them to release her was nothing compared to what she threw at the *Mal*.

Brutal. Punishingly dark. Immediately debilitating. Negative energy flowed out of her in a wave set to crash through any and all internal walls. Not even the strongest man surrounding them could shield against it. Even the demon had no defenses against it because her power overruled his.

Though she hadn't used her power like this in a very long time, she knew just how to make what was usually a force for good into a destructive force. Every fear, every terror, every imagined slight they'd ever felt came back at them like sharp-edged blades. It was the opposite of compassion and she knew she'd pay a price later but the situation was dire.

Everyone froze, demon included. She'd thought maybe the demon would be unaffected, simply because it didn't have emotions like humans. It was a creature filled with darkness.

Luckily for them, she was wrong.

The demon's expression was a rictus of pain. The longer she funneled her negative power outward, the worse it got. When it began to keen, the high-pitched sound made her shudder.

God, the agony. Her stomach flipped over in protest and she had to swallow down the urge to vomit and hold back the need to cry.

While she'd been focused on the demon, the *Mal* had dropped their guns and most were holding their heads in their hands, sobbing. The others had curled into protective balls on the ground. She imagined they were crying, as well.

She took the opportunity to look over her shoulder and found Den and Jacoby staring at her with what she imagined was horror. A crazy little voice inside her head whispered, "Guess you're not getting laid tonight," then began to laugh hysterically.

Pushing those thoughts out of her head, she blinked to erase the tears. "You two need to move. Now."

Neither of them responded right away but after a few seconds, Jacoby finally shook his head as if to clear it. It must have worked because he reached out to shake Den's shoulder.

"Can you hold them while you run?" Jacoby asked. Den seemed slower to respond but at least he wasn't curled in a fetal position on the ground. She'd managed to shield them somewhat.

"I don't know."

"Well, then let's find out."

He reached for her, but she drew away. If he touched her now, he'd be as infected as the *Mal* and the demon. And unable to run.

"I'll keep them incapacitated. You and Den get—"

"Not happening."

Den seemed to have shaken off his fear and was back to his old self. And if he was still a little pale beneath his tan, who could blame him. She was just as scary as any demon. A fact she'd managed to keep quiet for so many years. Amity knew, and a few of her other sister goddesses. It wasn't exactly something you spilled to potential bed partners, after all.

"Come on, Kari. Let's get moving. The car's not far. If you can hold them from a distance, or at least for a few more yards, we can get there."

So they didn't want to leave her behind? A rush of sweeter emotion nearly made her lose her grip on the dark. She actually had to blink back more tears.

"I can try. Just don't touch me. It makes it harder for me to keep you out of range."

Both men nodded then began to back away, motioning for her to follow.

It took an immense amount of concentration, but she managed to get her feet moving in the same direction as Den and Jacoby. She'd never before expended so much negative energy or used it as a weapon. She never wanted to have to do it again.

But this was her life and she wasn't going to give it up so easily.

By the time the men were out of sight, she was shaking with the effort and very nearly to the edge of her tolerance.

And before she finally blacked out, the last thing she remembered was Den's strong arms grabbing her before she hit the ground.

FIVE

Jacoby watched Den throw Kari over his shoulder then they both started to run.

He had no time to think, no time to wonder what the hell had just happened. He only knew they had to get to the car and get the hell out of here before those men and that demon regrouped and came after them.

He figured they'd be motivated as hell to get to Kari now that they knew what she could do.

He still couldn't believe she had that much power. The implications of that made him shake his head as they made it to the car.

Den ripped open the passenger door and carefully settled Kari in the back seat while Jacoby got behind the wheel and started the car. When Den slid into the passenger seat, Jacoby revved the engine and shot down the trail leading to the nearest paved road.

Since he knew they only had one place to go, he headed for the nearest road heading south. Since there was literally only one major road out of the area, he knew where he was going.

But that meant the *Mal* would be on their asses. He had to put enough miles between them and their pursuers so when they reached civilization and he attempted to lose them, they might have an actual shot at it.

With his foot heavy on the gas pedal, he had to keep his attention laser-focused on the road. It helped keep his mind off the scene they'd left behind. Den sat just as silently, gaze trained straight ahead. They drove in silence for at least half an hour, the radio filling in the dead space in the car. But finally, he couldn't keep quiet any longer.

"What the hell happened back there?"

It took Den a full minute to answer and, when he did, it wasn't an answer at all.

"Did you have any idea she had that much power?"

Jacoby shot Den a glare. "How the hell would I have known that?"

"Shit. I didn't— I'm not accusing you of anything. But holy hell..."

Yeah. Holy hell was an understatement. "Do you have any idea what she did?"

Out of the corner of his eye, he saw Den shake his head. "When she touched me, I felt like every single fear I'd ever had in my life hit me all at once. I wanted to curl in a ball and hide in a dark hole. I figure I got a pretty low dose. I can't imagine what she unleashed on them."

They both fell silent again, but Jacoby knew it wouldn't last.

"They're not gonna stop," Den said. "Christ, she put an even bigger target on her back."

"And made my sister an even bigger commodity."

"Shit." Den turned to stare at him. "*Fuck*. I didn't even think of that. *Vaffanculo*, I hope to hell the *lucani* got her out. We need to call."

"We can't. The phones have GPS—Fuck, so does the car."

He yanked the car to the side of the road and slammed on the brakes.

"What the hell—"

"We need to disable the fucking GPS so they can't track us."

"How the hell are we supposed to do that? Do you even know how—"

"I just need a minute."

Sucking in a deep breath, Jacoby attempted to calm his nerves. Yeah, it was pretty much a losing proposition, but it did help. A little. Okay, not that much but he didn't have time to fuck around. And no, he wasn't sure he could do this but it was either this or ditch the car and steal another.

You can do this. Just focus.

Closing his eyes, he put his hands on the dashboard and unleashed the magic he typically hid deep inside himself. The magic not even Den knew about.

It had become second nature to keep this secret, one only he and his sister knew. A secret she'd made him promise to keep to himself. To never use it unless his life was in danger. Because if the *Mal* found out what he could do, they'd use him for much worse than simple guard duty.

He had a vague notion that the GPS chip was located somewhere in the dash, so that's where he started. Using his magic like a bloodhound, he sent it into the car. Magic and technology didn't play nice together. Usually, you couldn't use one against the other and, if you tried, you ended up frustrated or worse, you burned out your magical powers for a certain period of time.

His father had once explained that technology was like a black hole that, when you attempted to affect it, the resulting explosion blew back on you. His father didn't have a clue. But Jacoby did, because of his rare talent. Technology wasn't a black hole. It was another form of magic. And Jacoby could control it.

He'd never heard of another person who could do what he could. He'd grown up being told by his sister to hide what he could do, to pretend he was less than what he was.

Now he had to use his power to save their asses.

No pressure at all.

From the electronics in the steering wheel, he followed the wiring into the dash and from there spread out, hoping like hell his connection to the electronics would lead him to where he needed to go. Magic was an imprecise art but it could be controlled and directed. Usually. Luckily for him, the car had a built-in navigation system. It'd make sense that the chip would be there.

And finally, he caught a break. As his *arus* passed by the other electronics, they gave off energy, some of which he could read. Understand was probably a better word to describe it. Whatever word you wanted to use, the end result was he could figure out what type of information that piece of technology was transmitting.

When he brushed up against a certain chip, the image he got in his head was maps. That had to be it. In the next second, he sent a bolt of energy directly to that chip and fried it.

When he opened his eyes, he turned to Den, staring at him with a steady gaze.

"Whatever you did, did it work?"

Shit. He'd never heard Den direct that tone at him. He'd only ever heard his friend use it against people he didn't trust, which was pretty much everyone else. Everyone except Jacoby.

"Den—"

"Not now." Den shook his head and glanced over the back seat, to where Kari was still out cold. "Just get us back on the road. We need to get far enough away from here to dump this car and get another one. Can you hotwire a car with your gift?"

"I've never had to, but it shouldn't be a problem."

"Then the first car you see that won't raise an immediate alarm, stop and we'll take it."

An added level of tension descended when Den fell silent. Jacoby kept his attention on the road and his mouth shut. He knew Den was pissed but he also knew his friend well enough to know Den was working through his anger and, when he was ready, he'd ask questions.

And Jacoby would try to answer them.

"So this gift..." Den finally spoke fifteen minutes later. "How long have you had it?"

Jacoby breathed a sigh of relief before he answered. "Since birth, I think. My parents always had trouble with computers and electronics in the house. They kept getting fucked up. Same for the TVs. My dad wasn't home much so he didn't notice or he didn't care. Or my sister just got good at covering for me. Either way, we managed to keep it hidden until I could control it."

"Does anyone else know?"

He shook his head. "Emelia knew if anyone found out, the *Mal* would take me and she'd never see me again. She helped me control it, helped me hide it. I've never heard of anyone else who can do the things I can do. I'm not saying I'm the only one out there. I'm just saying, if there are other people with the same ability, they're either hiding it or suppressing it."

Den didn't respond for almost a full second. When he did, his question was unexpected.

"So your magic disrupts technology. What makes your power different?"

"I can control it."

"How the hell did you manage to keep that a secret? Jesus, my parents were all over me about my Gift, even though it's barely usable. It's not like I can talk to animals. I can just barely influence them. Sometimes it works, sometimes it doesn't. And when it does, I can maybe understand what the hell deer are thinking or if there's a predator in the area."

Jacoby knew this. He and Den had been friends for years. Which just made Jacoby feel even more shitty for not telling Den. "I'm sorry. My sister made me swear as a kid never to tell anyone. Maybe I was a little too paranoid. Maybe I took it too far. Maybe—"

"You did what you thought was best. You don't have to apologize. That's not..." Den paused then sighed and ran a hand through his hair. "It's just a shock. Just let me work through it." He huffed out a dry laugh. "Just when you think you know everything there is to know about someone..."

Jacoby felt a weight lift off his shoulders. He'd hated keeping this secret from Den. Had never wanted to but his sister's fear had worked a little too well, apparently.

"So *no one* else knows?"

Shaking his head, he navigated through the increasing darkness of the night. No street lights lit this stretch of road and the wildlife population in the area was dense. He didn't want to accidentally hit anything.

"No."

"No one's ever suspected?"

"Maybe." He shrugged. "I don't know. If they did, it wasn't enough to investigate. Besides, as far as I know, no one else has this kind of a Gift so no one's looking for it."

More silence, this time less filled with tension.

Den sighed, staring at him outright now. "We should go to Vegas. Christ, we'd be rich."

It took a second for Den's words to sink in then Jacoby began to laugh. Because that was the real Den. The one who managed to make him smile when he threatened to become too damn morose.

"I've considered it a few times but I don't use it enough to make it work like that."

"Then I guess we need to get you to practice. Christ, Jack, with a little effort, there's no telling what you'd be able to do."

"Do with what?"

Kari's voice sounded weak but alert. Jacoby allowed himself to take his eyes off the road for a few brief seconds to check on her in the rearview while Den swung around in his seat.

"How are you feeling? Are you okay? What the hell happened back there?"

Jacoby winced at the demand in Den's voice. Kari was a goddess, not just an ordinary woman to order around. She demanded a level of respect.

So he reached over and punched Den on the arm.

"For fuck's sake, Den." He kept his voice low. "Watch your godsdamn mouth."

Den didn't even bother to glare at him, just kept his attention firmly on Kari, who yawned and almost made him drive off the side of the road when he caught a glimpse of her as she stretched.

Fuck.

He was just as bad as Den. At least he didn't broadcast his lust as clearly as Den. Not that she seemed to mind. Yeah, he really didn't need to be thinking about shit like that right now. They had a long drive and he need to keep his attention focused. And not on her.

"It's okay, Jacoby. He's worried and that's my fault. I didn't mean to worry you."

Another glance in the rearview and he caught her smiling that sleepy, sexy-as-fuck smile that made him want to climb into the back seat and take her hard and fast. And then watch Den do the same.

He shook his head. This woman—no, this *goddess* gave him

all sorts of ideas he'd never had before and he couldn't tell if they originated from him or from her.

And did it really matter?

He only knew he needed to get her to the *lucani* and make sure his sister was safe. Then maybe he could get his head back on straight and figure out what the hell he was gonna do now that he'd burned the only life he knew to the ground.

"Then what the hell happened back there?" Den asked again. "You scared the shit out of us."

"I am *so* sorry about that." Her voice held a deep sorrow that made Jacoby want to wrap his arms around her and pull her close. "I didn't mean to hurt you—"

"I'm not talking about what you did to us. I'm taking about you hurting yourself."

Silence from the back seat. Jacoby glanced in the mirror to make sure she was okay. Not crying. Crying would be bad. If Den had made her cry, he'd have to beat him. She wasn't. At least, he didn't think she was. She looked mostly confused.

"You're not afraid of me?"

"Why would we be afraid of you?" Jacoby asked when Den seemed to have lost his voice.

"Because of the way I used my power against you. It was the only way I could think of to get you to release me. I didn't want you to be touching me when I turned it on the *Mal*."

"Shit, no. I'm not angry about that. I'm pissed off that you hurt yourself. Are you okay?"

"Yes, I'm fine."

In the rearview, Jacoby saw her lips curve in a smile and he finally breathed a sigh of relief. He hadn't realized how much stress he'd been holding until it lifted.

"So what happened, Kari?" Jacoby glanced into the review again because he couldn't help himself. "Why'd you pass out?"

He heard her shifting around the seat behind them a second

before she put one hand on his shoulder and the other on Den's. Her touch sent electricity sparking through his body, causing his hands to clench around the wheel. He wanted to reach for her, but the twisting road required both hands on the wheel.

Den grabbed her hand and pressed a kiss to the palm. It should've made Jacoby uncomfortable. Why it didn't wasn't something he wanted to explore right now. Instead, he pressed the gas pedal a little closer to the floor as they hit a relatively straight stretch of road. The faster they got to the wolves, the better he'd feel. They were too exposed out here on the road.

And he didn't want anything to happen to her.

"I overextended myself. I haven't had to use that much power in so long that I forgot how to regulate it. I'm afraid I might have caused some of those men serious damage."

She sounded so upset but he shook his head. "You know what they have planned for you. Don't feel sorry for anything you do to them to keep yourself safe."

"I understand that. It also goes against everything I am."

"Yeah, well, don't do it again." Den's tone gentled some but not much. "We'll handle the *Mal*."

"You can't handle the demon."

"You didn't give us the chance."

Den's voice rumbled with anger and Jacoby shot him a glace to get him to shut the fuck up.

"I'm not trying to be mean, but you couldn't have handled the demon." Her hand gripped his shoulder tighter and he had to resist the urge to put his hand over hers. "And this one had a hell of a lot of power. I'd love to know what it was doing with the *Mal*. I haven't seen one in centuries and I know they don't normally walk freely on this plane."

This plane. Tinia's teat, that rattled him. Theoretically, he knew there were other worlds, realms, planes of existence, whatever the hell you wanted to call them. But they'd always been more idea than reality.

Now... Damn, he'd actually seen a demon. From hell. Aitás was much more real now than it'd been before. It was going to take some time to come to terms with that.

Says the man who can interface with machinery.

He shot a look at Den and figured they both had pretty much the same look on their faces. Shock. Disbelief. A whole lot of "holy shit" and "what the fuck."

Den was the first to find his voice.

"We had no idea the *Mal* are working with a demon."

"I know that." Kari's voice coated the darkness inside and out of the car with warmth. And made Jacoby's cock swell against the zipper of his pants. "This demon's no low-level grunt, either. He's hierarchy. And that's a whole other worry on its own."

"Why does that make a difference?" Den asked.

Before she could answer, she yawned. "Because it means Charun is either working with the *Mal* or he doesn't know what his minions are doing. And that's probably worse than anything else. Without Charun to keep them under control, the upper-echelon demons are brilliant and bloodthirsty and power-hungry. And they have absolutely no conscience."

Jacoby shook his head, trying to think. "So why the hell are they working with the *Mal?*"

Kari's hand tightened on his shoulder. "I don't know but whatever it is, it's not good."

"What did he say to you?" Den asked. "It was talking to you, wasn't it?"

"It was taunting me, telling me how obsolete and useless I was. It didn't seem to have a purpose, unless it just wanted to piss me off."

"Can you think of any reason it would want you?"

She fell silent for several long seconds, her index finger tapping a steady beat against his shirt. "No. I don't have any idea why they'd want me. Unless..."

"Unless what?"

Jacoby couldn't chance looking in the mirror. The road had started to twist again as they began to come out of the mountains.

"Maybe they want what Charun wanted. To be free of Aitás. They can only spend a limited amount of time on this plane or they risk being wiped from existence. They were created to serve Charun and given limited powers, so they wouldn't be able to revolt or escape..."

She paused and Jacoby realized why immediately.

"If they take your power, will they be able to cross through to this plane more easily and stay longer?"

She removed her hand and slid back into her seat and he immediately missed her touch.

"Possibly. Probably, yes. It makes sense. What I can't figure out is why Charun would allow it. He wants out but he knows the demons can't be allowed to roam. They're too unstable, too violent."

"Maybe he doesn't care," Den said.

"Maybe he doesn't know." Jacoby shrugged. "I guess it doesn't matter. The end result is the same. They're working with the *Mal* and we need to figure out how to fight that."

"I'm not sure there is any way to fight them." Kari sounded much more somber than she usually did. And tired. "I need to talk to Amity and the rest of my sisters. We need..." another yawn that made her sigh, "to figure out how to send them back to Aitás."

He and Den exchanged a worried glance as she yawned again.

"We've still got about five hours of driving before we get to the wolves, why don't you stretch out and take a nap?" Jacoby suggested. Den would've demanded, which was why Jacoby had spoken up.

"We'll wake you if anything happens," Den added. "You look tired."

Jacoby winced. He knew better than to tell a woman she looked less than perfect. Den should, too.

Kari chuckled. "Yes, I'm sure I do. I feel tired. But I think I should be awake if they catch up to us."

"Aren't you wiped out, magically speaking?"

"I am, actually." She paused. "But..."

Jacoby knew she wanted to say something else. He didn't know why she would hesitate. What wasn't she telling them?

"But what?" Den prompted. "What's wrong?"

"Oh, nothing's wrong. Nothing that a good long sleep would cure. Or..."

"Or what?" Den's frustration coated every word. "Spit it out."

"Well, sex is always a good way to recharge my battery."

Jacoby's mouth actually fell open seconds before his libido leaped at the suggestion in her words and threatened to make him pull to the side of the road and climb over the back seat.

He couldn't chance a look in the rearview but he did glance at Den, who looked just as dumbstruck as he was sure he did. But in the blink of an eye, his expression flooded with lust.

Holy shit.

Did she mean— Could she possibly want—

"Well, you both don't have to answer all at once. I can't believe I scared you into silence."

Her tone held amusement, but Jacoby thought he heard a little hurt as well. And that was unacceptable. But...

Holy shit. Did she just want him to pull over to the side of the road? Or did she just want Den to crawl into the backseat?

Jacoby wasn't sure he'd be able to keep the car on the road if he had to listen to them—

"As much as we would love to take you up on that offer," Den had to clear his throat before he could continue, "I think we need to get to the wolves as soon as possible."

Her sigh made Jacoby struggle to swallow a groan. She sounded so...disappointed.

Oh, fuck. Join the club, babe.

"I suppose you're right. Okay, I guess I'll just stretch out here for a little while and—"

"But as soon as we get to the wolves," Den continued, "all bets are off."

He couldn't help himself. Jacoby had to look in the rearview.

Her smile, sleepy and sexy as fuck, threatened to obliterate his concentration. His cock swelled, threatening to split his zipper and his hands tightened on the wheel hard enough to make it creak.

"Then I guess I have something to look forward to." Her gaze met his in the mirror before sliding toward Den. "Drive safely. Wake me if you need to."

Jacoby heard her shift around on the seat then silence. Which held for at least ten minutes before Den finally cracked.

"She's out. Jack—"

"We need to ditch this car and find something else."

Den's heavy sigh filled the front seat. "We need to talk about this."

No, they really didn't. At least, not now. "We can talk about it after we find another car."

"I need to know if you're gonna be okay with this."

"*This* being a threesome? We don't need to talk about it now."

"But we *are* going to talk about it.

Jacoby kept his mouth shut and his concentration focused on the road.

"Yeah, we'll talk."

Jacoby just didn't know what the hell he was going to say.

SIX

Den practically bit his tongue in half to keep from prodding Jacoby into saying something more.

But he knew his friend, and he knew it would take Jacoby a while to process what he was thinking and feeling. And, for the first time in a very long time, he had no idea what Jacoby was thinking. Usually, they were on the same page. Usually, whatever Jacoby said, Den agreed with and vice versa.

Not now.

Den wanted Kari with a grinding ache that had only intensified the more time they spent together. He wanted to strip her naked and give her anything she wanted. She wanted both of them. And, while Den had no problem with that, he was pretty sure Jacoby did.

They'd never shared a woman, even though their tastes generally tended toward similar women. Women whose personalities weren't overblown or loud. Quiet. Gentle. Stable. Kari wasn't any of those things. She said whatever came into her head, expected you to do the same and never backed down. She could be quiet but she was never cowed.

Hell, they'd been holding her against her will for the past

three months but she'd never been pissed off at them. She'd smiled and flirted and made Den have to fight to keep his libido in check. She'd never tried to escape, although he now knew that if she'd wanted to leave, she would've walked out the door and neither of them would've been able to stop her.

She had much more power than he'd suspected, probably more than anyone had known. And he'd make sure no one ever took that away from her. At least until she was ready to give it up on her own.

To Jacoby's sister.

"You're thinking so damn hard, you're giving me a headache. Give it a break, will you?"

Jacoby's voice threw him out of his thoughts and Den turned to stare at him.

"I thought you wanted to wait to have this talk."

Den kept his voice down, not wanting to wake Kari, but he heard something in Jacoby's voice that made him draw in a deep breath. He guessed he should've expected this. Jacoby had a much shorter fuse than Den.

"It's been an hour. I've had enough time to think. And I think it's a bad idea."

Shit, really? He'd lost an hour in thought. "What's a bad idea? Do you mean going to the wolves? Trusting them with my mom and your sister? Or the fact that a *goddess* wants to sleep with us? Pick one, Jack."

"You know which one. Don't be an ass. I'm taking myself out of the equation."

Den stared at him, shaking his head. "Just like that? Do you really think you have the final say?"

"I still have free will. I don't have to fall in bed with her just because she snaps her fingers."

"Are you telling me you don't want her? Because I know that's bullshit."

Jack's jaw tightened until Den thought the bone might crack. "I'm saying I don't think I want to share her."

"So you want her for yourself?"

Another pause, this one longer. "Of course I do."

"Then it's me you have a problem with."

Now Jacoby's hands tightened on the steering while until his knuckles went white. "I don't have a problem with you. Don't fucking put words in my mouth."

"Then say what the fuck you mean. I'm getting sick of trying to read your mind."

"I'm trying to save our fucking friendship. You've been lusting after her for months."

"So have you."

"But you can handle her, Den. To you, she's a woman. To me, she's still a goddess. I was raised to believe they were untouchable. And I might not be able to get beyond that."

"But we've lived with her for the past three months. You know she's so much more than a myth. She's a woman, too. Flesh and blood and desire."

"And that's why I can't even consider it. She's not just a woman to me. She's an ideal. And I might need to believe in that more than I believe in the woman."

Well, shit. This was an angle Den hadn't even considered and it made him shake his head.

"Then you need to tell her."

"I plan to. I just didn't want you to fight me about it when I do. And as soon as my sister's safe, I'll leave."

"What do you mean?"

"You know what I mean."

Yeah, Den was afraid he did. And that was a whole other problem. They'd been a team for the past ten years. Den knew he could function without Jacoby. He just didn't want to.

"No. There's a way to handle this that doesn't require us to split up."

"Well, when you figure that out, let me know."

Another silence fell and this time, neither of them broke it for a half hour. They'd finally gotten into a more populated area and they needed to ditch this car for another.

Since it was three a.m. on a Sunday morning, they decided a used car lot would be their best target. No one would probably notice the car was gone until Monday morning. By that time, they should be in den territory and the car would be long gone.

It wasn't hard to find the right car. A gray Honda with a few years on it, old enough that the electronics wouldn't be a problem. Although with Jacoby's powers...

Yeah, that still made Den want to hit something, but he managed to keep his mouth shut while they pulled into the dark parking lot and made quick work of getting into the Honda and getting it started.

Then Den carefully maneuvered Kari out of their old car and into the new. She never woke, which worried Den. But not enough for him to insist they wake her. They'd be at the den in a few more hours and would wake her when they got there. Until then, he and Jacoby would have to deal with each other.

"Jack...look, we need to stick together. The *Mal*'s going to come after us and we're going to need to watch each other's backs."

"Don't you think I know that? I'm trying to stay the fuck out of your way."

"Why would I want you to do that?"

"So you and Kari can be together."

"But she doesn't just want me. She wants both of us."

Jacoby's jaw clenched so hard, Den swore he heard his teeth crack. "And that doesn't bother you? Honestly?"

"The only person I'd even consider making this work with is you."

"And if I can't get past having to share her with you...what then?"

"Then we'll working something out. Right now, we just need to focus on getting to the den without getting caught. I'm not sure they know exactly where we're going but they probably have a pretty good idea. We need to figure out how to get there without getting caught."

"Do you even know where we're going? I mean, I have a general idea, but I don't figure we're going to be able to just walk through the front door."

"We can worry about that when we get closer. Right now, I think we need to figure out how to contact them and let them know we're on our way."

"I don't think Cole's going to post his phone number on Facebook."

Den was glad to hear Jacoby somewhat back to his normal, occasionally sarcastic self. But he was right. They'd been counting on having Kari guide them. But she was still down for the count and he didn't want to disturb her unless they absolutely had to. But as they got closer to Allentown in Pennsylvania, Den knew they were going to have to do it because they needed direction.

"We need to find a motel, one that isn't going to ask a lot of questions and has separate entrances." Den pointed to the nearest exit off the turnpike. "We need to get her into a room and I don't want anyone to see me carry her inside. That's a sure way to have someone call the cops on us and we don't need to deal with that."

"No-tell motel it is." Jacoby headed for the off ramp. "How the hell are we going to wake her?"

"Let's worry about that once we have a room."

WHERE A GODDESS BELONGS   85

They found what they were looking for after only a few minutes. A slightly rundown, one-story motel in a U-shape with doors that opened out to the parking lot.

While Jacoby went inside to pay and get the key, Den slid into the back seat and attempted to wake Kari. Even in the gray light of dawn, he could see her color wasn't good. She looked pale and had dark circles under eyes.

When Jacoby returned with an actual key on a numbered tag, he looked into the back seat, eyes narrowing when he saw Den with her in his arms.

"Fuck, she doesn't look good." Sliding into the driver's seat, he drove them around to the back of the building on the left. "I asked the manager for the room farthest from the highway."

Luckily, the room opened onto a rear parking lot where only one other car was parked. Three doors with numbers faced a wooded lot at the rear. Jacoby wasted no time getting out of the car and opening the door while Den picked up Kari and handed her to Jacoby, who'd come back to help. It only took seconds to get inside and close and lock the door behind them.

As Jacoby laid Kari on one of the two queen beds in the surprisingly large space, Den checked out the room. There was a small window in the bathroom that Kari could possibly squeeze through if she had to but otherwise, the only way in or out was the front door or the large window beside it.

Den made sure the curtains covered it completely before he went to the bed, where Jacoby sat on the side staring down at Kari, holding one of her hands in his.

"She's out cold." Jacoby looked over at him and shook his head, his expression dark and worried. "I tried to wake her but I'm not having any luck. You don't think she's in a coma, do you?"

Den sat on the other side of the bed, grabbing her other

hand feeling for a pulse. "I don't think so. Her pulse is strong. I think she's just wiped out from using her power."

"Did you have any idea she could still do that?"

"No. Let's hope no one else knows."

"How are we gonna figure out how to get to the den?"

Den looked at Jacoby and waited until he caught his gaze. "Kiss her."

Heat flashed into Jacoby's eyes before he blinked and wiped it away. "Don't fucking push me."

"She needs to recharge. And she's gonna need both of us to do it. You probably have more raw power than I do, considering what you can do."

"You've got a godsdamn Goddess Gift, Den."

"Which isn't anywhere near as powerful as what you can do. Kiss her, Jack. Stop being a dick. This isn't about what we want any more. It's about what she *needs*."

Jacoby stared back at him for what had to be a full minute before he sucked in a breath and turned back to Kari. Then he leaned forward and pressed his mouth against her.

Den tried to watch with a clinical eye, tried not to think about what this woman, this goddess, wanted them to do to her.

He was worried about her and that worry was a nagging ache in his gut. But he also wanted her and that desire burned through his blood. If she were awake and Jacoby was kissing her, where would he fit into the scene? He had a few ideas but the main one involved him with his head between her legs, licking her until she came.

Fuck.

As he shook the thought out of his head, he focused on Jacoby, who was doing nothing more than pressing his lips against hers.

"Seriously, man? That's how you kiss a woman?"

Jacoby broke the connection, sat back and stared at him. "She's out cold. I feel like a fucking creeper."

"You're not doing anything she doesn't want. She *asked* for this. Now fucking kiss her like you mean it."

Jacoby stared at him for several long seconds, but Den wasn't backing down. Jacoby knew he was right. He was over-thinking. Again.

"Kiss her, Jack. Show her how you really feel about her."

Jacoby took a deep breath and leaned forward again. He went slow, pressed his lips against hers just enough to let her know he was there. Den could tell he was still holding back and was about to say something but then Jacoby moved his head. He angled it a little differently, enough to make her lips part.

Now, Jacoby kissed her with slow deliberation, like he'd thought out every move and was putting a plan into action. But he also kissed her with an increasing passion.

Moving his lips over hers, Jacoby slid one hand up her arm to cup her head in his palm and tilt her chin up a little more. When Jacoby drew back for a breath, Den saw Kari's lips had parted, and her cheeks had a little more color than before. At least, he thought they did. Her breathing also seemed to be coming a little faster but that could just be wishful thinking on his part.

What wasn't wishful thinking was the thickening of his cock in his jeans. That was most definitely happening. Damn, maybe Jacoby was right. Maybe this was totally fucked up. And maybe it was exactly what she needed.

When Jacoby bent to kiss her again, Den could have sworn he felt her hand grip his. Because he couldn't be sure, he sat as still as possible and watched Jacoby kiss her with a little more passion.

And now he knew she tightened her hand on his. At the same time, he heard Jacoby groan as Kari moved her head and responded to his kiss. With a tight hold on Den's hand, she released Jacoby's hand so she could curve it around his neck and hold on. Jacoby didn't seem in any hurry to stop now that he'd started.

Their kiss made all the air in the room disappear. And Den wanted in on the action. Instead, he forced himself to keep his distance. Didn't want Jacoby to freak and run.

But damn, their kiss began to take on an erotic edge that made Den feel like a voyeur. He could kind of understand why Jacoby might be weirded out by watching another man kiss or fuck a woman he wanted.

Then again, Den had never seen anything so fucking hot in his life. He'd never seen Jacoby kiss a woman before, but he could tell his friend had had a lot of practice. Den hoped he wouldn't pale in comparison.

Jacoby seemed to have forgotten all about him, kissing her with an increasing fervor. His lips moved over hers with purpose then parting hers so he could slip his tongue between them. As their tongues connected, he heard her moan and now her hand practically crushed his.

The heat between them scalded him.

He didn't know how long Jacoby and Kari held that kiss but when they finally separated, they both panted like it'd been days since they'd been able to breathe. Finally, her eyes opened. And Den breathed a huge sigh of relief.

"Kari. Are you okay?"

She didn't answer immediately. She took a second to smile up at Jacoby, who looked dazed. Probably a lot like Den had looked after he'd kissed her in the kitchen. Finally, she turned to Den, her smile still in place, lips kiss swollen and so fucking enticing.

"I think so." She moved to sit up but only got halfway before immediately lying back down again. "Then again, maybe I'll just stay here a few more minutes."

"Shit." Jacoby stood so fast, he probably gave himself vertigo. "We need to get you to the den. We probably shouldn't have stopped."

Kari grabbed his hand and stopped him from moving away. "No, you were right to stop. You need me awake to find the den and I needed a little...help waking up."

Her smile was weak, but it was there. Den breathed a little easier. Jacoby, however, looked ready to combust. And not in a good way.

"Just tell us where we need to go then you can get some sleep. We'll figure out the rest."

Her smile looked a little sad. "It's not just a matter of an address. You need help with the wards or you'll never find the place."

"Can't we contact someone, have them meet us?"

Gee, could Jacoby act any more eager to get rid of her? Didn't he see how her expression dimmed?

He wanted to take a swing at his best friend and tell him to shape the fuck up. But he didn't want to do it in front of Kari. She had enough to worry about without having him and Jacoby at each other's throats. But the first time Den got him alone, all bets were off.

"If you'd like, you can drop me off at Sal's and I'll be out of your hair."

Okay, maybe he would take one swing right now for making her sound like that, like she was defeated.

"That's not what I meant. And it's not what I want." Jacoby's jaw tightened until Den thought it might crack. "Dammit. I don't want to get rid of you. I just want you to be safe."

"Well, you have a pretty damn funny way of showing it."

There was a little heat in her words now, a tone he'd never heard her use before. She was getting pissed.

Den thought about stepping in but decided he'd sit back and watch them go at it. Jacoby was an adult. He could fight his own battles. And he was pretty sure Kari didn't need much help to defend herself. At least not against Jacoby.

Because Den was pretty sure Jack didn't really want to fight with her. He wanted much more than a kiss and, if it took a shouting match to get there, well, Den would enjoy the show.

HOW MUCH FARTHER *do I have to push Jacoby until he kisses me again?*

Kari still had a power hangover and needed to recharge. Sure, she could use more sleep and a few cheeseburgers and chocolate shakes. But sex was so much better when it came to restoring her energy.

Jacoby was proving to be a stubborn case, though. When she'd started to come out of her fugue, she'd been thrilled to find Jacoby kissing her. Not that she wouldn't have been just as thrilled with Den but Den wasn't resisting her as hard as Jacoby.

Den had been ready to do her in the kitchen if they'd had time. She was pretty sure if she asked, he'd crawl in bed with her right now and give her exactly what she wanted. But what she really wanted was both. And that was proving much harder than it normally did.

Especially with Jacoby scowling down at her and looking like he wanted to run. Maybe she shouldn't have let her frustration show with her last statement. Maybe she should've continued to flirt and cajole and wait until he came around. And maybe she would've had to wait until the demon actually caught up to her again before he'd give in and give her what she wanted.

With a sigh, she shook her head and let her eyes close as she rested her head back on the pillow again.

Maybe she did need to sleep a little more. She still felt groggy.

You know what would help with that. Sex.

Of course, there was still another man in the room.

Opening her eyes, she turned to find Den watching her from the other side of the bed. Den never really said much. She had the feeling he allowed Jacoby to speak for both of them most of the time. Not because he didn't have an opinion or the intellect but because he probably thought Jacoby explained things better than he could.

Which wasn't true. Den could express himself just as well as Jacoby. He just did it with many fewer words. He was a man of action. And right now, she needed some.

"Den." Her voice made his gaze narrow on her. "Will you give me what I need? Jacoby doesn't want to be helpful."

"I'll give you whatever you want."

She smiled, a familiar heat flowing through her veins. "I'm not asking for much. Just sex."

The hunger already present in Den's gaze flared as his lips flattened and his hand tightened on hers. He hadn't released her the entire time she'd been arguing with Jacoby.

Fuck it. Den wanted her and she wanted him just as much as she wanted Jacoby. In her mind, they were equals. Not two halves of a whole but two entities. Separately, they made her hot. If she had them together, she might spontaneously combust.

She was willing to take the chance, of course, but if Jacoby wasn't...

"Then I'd like you to kiss me."

Now he did glance up at Jacoby but he wasn't asking

permission. He was giving his friend one last chance. She didn't check to see Jacoby's reaction. She remained focused on Den, who, after a few, short seconds, looked away from Jacoby and back to her.

In the next second, he pressed his mouth against hers and took her breath away.

She hadn't gotten the chance to experience Jacoby's kiss from the beginning and regretted that she couldn't entice him into kissing her again. But Den more than made up what she'd missed and then some.

Where Jacoby's kiss had been almost worshipful, Den kissed her like a man kissed a woman. Not a goddess, but a woman he craved. A woman he wanted to throw on the bed and fuck until neither of them could breathe and both of them wanted to sleep for the next two days.

That's the kind of sex she craved. And Den was probably the only person she'd ever met who knew who she was and wanted to give it to her anyway.

His lips moved on hers with a force that stole her breath and she responded with a heat all her own.

Tinia's teat. It'd been so long since she'd let herself get lost in a kiss, let a man take her under with just the heat of his mouth and a talented tongue. Would he use that tongue elsewhere if she asked? She was pretty sure he would.

Letting the slight hurt from Jacoby fall away, she concentrated instead on Den, who wanted her regardless of who and what she was. She could sense his desire, sense the need he had for her. It communicated itself in the waves of heat coming from his body and the intense longing battering at her senses.

Responding to that need, she opened her mouth to him and allowed his tongue to slip between her lips and tangle with her own. His taste exploded on her tongue, making her moan.

Lifting her arms, she wrapped them around his back then

sank her fingers into the silky hair that lay just over his nape. She'd been longing for weeks to put her hands in that hair, to feel it against her palms...and between her thighs as he went down on her.

The image made lust flash through her body and she tilted her head to get a better angle on his mouth. This... Yes, this was what she needed. She felt her power begin to rejuvenate, to course through her veins and make her feel more like herself again.

A low moan escaped her, and Den must've taken that as a sign that she wanted more. Oh hell, yes, she wanted more. So much more.

Exerting the slightest bit of pressure, she let Den know she wanted him to come closer. He didn't hesitate. Settling his hands on either side of her head, he leaned over, pressing her head back into the pillow and opening her mouth even farther.

And then he let loose. His mouth moved over hers with a purpose, teasing and coaxing, making her feel as if she was the only person in his world right now. As if he only had one purpose in mind and that was to make her feel like a goddess. Like she hadn't in so very long.

Her hands tightened in his hair, trying to tug him even closer but she wasn't sure that was possible. Unless they lost a few layers of clothes. And oh, yes, that's exactly what she wanted. Naked skin pressed against naked skin. Damp, heated flesh clinging.

She already felt her skin slicken, especially between her thighs. Her nipples had pebbled to tight points that ached for hands to caress them. Jacoby's hands, preferably, while Den let his linger between her legs.

Her hips arched up, the ache between them growing with every second. Such a wonderful ache. As his tongue lashed against hers, she felt the ache expand from between her thighs to her gut. So hot and unlike anything she'd experienced in years.

It'd been so long since she'd let herself fully enjoy sex. For so long, she'd been using random men to slake her hunger, mostly *eteri*. Men without magic who did nothing to refill the well of her power.

This man would do more than refill it. And together, he and Jacoby could—

No. Apparently, that wasn't going to happen. Unfortunately.

Den chose that moment to pull back, as if he'd sensed her attention begin to waver. He looked down into her eyes, the ice-blue of his now burning bright. Promising so much.

But she couldn't help herself. Call her greedy. She looked to her side.

And found Jacoby watching them with a hunger he did nothing to conceal. He'd moved to stand against the wall across from the bed, arms crossed over his chest. He didn't look torn now. He looked intrigued and turned on.

Stifling a smile, she let their gazes connect. She could make this work.

Moving one hand to Den's shoulder, she urged him to put his mouth on her neck, which he did immediately. Opening his mouth, he lightly sucked on her skin, creating a small sting, which he soothed with his tongue. Her eyes started to close but she forced them open, maintaining contact with Jacoby.

The connection held as Den kissed his way down her throat to her collarbone, exposed by the wide neckline of her shirt. She wasn't wearing a bra and her nipples poked against the soft cotton, aching for touch.

As if Den had read her mind, he brought one hand up to cup her left breast, his thumb and forefinger pinching the nipple between them almost to the point of pain. It felt so damn good, she wanted to close her eyes and drift in her arousal. Instead, she forced herself to watch Jacoby.

But his attention had drifted to Den's hand. And that was okay, too. Watching Jacoby watch Den pleasure her ramped up her arousal.

Sucking in a deep breath when she realized her lungs burned for the lack of oxygen, she arched her back, trying to make Den handle her with more force. Even though he didn't treat her like a porcelain doll, as a lot of other men did, he was aware enough of his strength to be cautious of using too much of it. His hand molded and shaped her breast but it wasn't enough to give her the sensation she wanted. She needed more.

"I'm not going to break. Harder, Den."

His head lifted from where he'd been biting her earlobe and he stared into her eyes.

"I don't want to hurt you."

His voice made all the tiny hairs on her body stand. So deep. And she heard his own arousal in the rough tone beneath. As if he was starting to lose control.

Yes, please. That's exactly what I want.

"You won't. Trust me. I want it."

His hand tightened on her and she wasn't sure if it was involuntary or not but it was what she needed. Moaning, she arched even more, her hands reaching above her for the headboard so she could arch even higher and harder into his hands.

Suddenly, he sat up, taking his hands away.

No, no, no.

About to protest, she snapped her lips closed when he grabbed the hem of her shirt and lifted it up her body and over her head.

Oh yes.

Her hair fell around her face in a mess, but Den's hands reached it before she could, brushing it out of her eyes before running his fingers through it to the ends. He let it fall from his fingers and over her breasts. The sensation of her own hair against her nipples made her shiver. And when Den brushed his fingers across her breasts, he pushed her hair away there, as well.

Every sensation was heightened, every nerve ending tingling with anticipation. Of what, she wasn't sure yet. She honestly didn't know if Den was going to make love to her or not. She certainly hoped so but she still wasn't sure he'd go that far with Jacoby in the room.

"You're fucking beautiful."

Her lips curved. "Thank you. I appreciate the compliment."

"Don't you agree, Jack? Isn't she the most beautiful woman you've ever seen?"

Den's gaze was glued to her body, watching as he pressed her breasts together, thumbs flicking her hard nipples. As if he might be imagining his cock thrusting between them.

Her thighs clenched on a wave of lust so powerful, she almost missed Jacoby's response.

She wasn't sure he'd answer at all but when he did, he left her with no doubt that he wanted her just as much as Den.

"Yes. She is."

She turned to Jacoby, whose gaze was locked on her breasts.

"Then why don't you join us?"

She held out her hand, steeling herself for his rejection. He didn't take it right away, but he didn't walk away either. After several long seconds, his gaze lifted to meet hers.

"I'm not sure I can give you what you want."

"How will you know if you never ask me what I want?"

Den returned his attention to her breasts, continuing to play with her nipples, trying to drive her to distraction, apparently. And it was working. But she was determined not to let Jacoby walk away without a fight.

His gaze slipped from hers to watch Den again. Out of the

corner of her eye, she saw Den lean forward a second before he put his mouth over one nipple. She sucked in a sharp breath as a wave of electricity shot from her breasts to her clit, making her sex clench with need. Her back arched again and she had to fight to keep her eyes open. Den's single-minded focus threatened to fracture her attention and she moaned, writhing against him, searching for satisfaction.

Jacoby took a step toward the bed. Her lungs worked to keep her body supplied with oxygen but it felt like a losing battle. Hell, having both of them at the same time might actually be more than she could handle at the moment. That should have been a sobering thought.

Instead, it exhilarated her. She'd never felt so overwhelmed and near the edge before and it thrilled her.

Reaching for Jacoby with one hand, she sank the other into the longer hair at Den's nape and held on for the ride.

JACOBY WASN'T sure which way was up anymore. Ten minutes ago, he'd been convinced he couldn't do this, couldn't give her what she wanted. He hadn't thought he'd be able to share Kari with another man, not even one he trusted as much as Den.

He'd never thought he'd want to watch another man make love to a woman. Now...he'd never been so turned on in his life.

Watching Den, watching her respond to him... Every nerve ending in his body felt energized, every inch of his skin burned like he was on fire.

His hands clenched into fists at his sides, attempting not to reach out and touch her, even though that's all he wanted to do. He wanted to put his hands on her breasts, to feel her nipples peak against his skin. Wanted to test the weight of those mounds in his palms and squeeze them until she cried out from his touch.

He wanted her to cry out while he had his hands on her and he wanted to kiss her as she moaned into his mouth. Now, her hand tightened on his as she closed her eyes while Den sucked her nipples into his mouth and made her arch her back as she sought more contact.

He didn't realize he'd taken another step closer until his knees hit the side of the bed. If he wanted to, he could kneel beside her, lean over and kiss her. The need became a nagging ache in his gut until he could resist no longer.

As if Den could read his mind, he began to drag his mouth lower, down to her stomach. Getting out of Jacoby's way.

Kari's eyes opened as Den moved, looking down before glancing up at Jacoby. Their gazes met and held for several long seconds before he lowered his head and kissed her.

And holy fuck, if he thought their earlier kiss had been hot, this one was off the charts.

That, more than anything, cut through the veil of indecision that'd been hovering over him. He was going to take what he wanted and damn the consequences. He could tell himself he was doing this for her but he'd be lying. Or, at least, only partly.

He wanted her any way he could get her. And if he had to share her, at least it was with Den, the only person in the world he trusted.

Cupping her head in his hands, he lifted her toward him, turning her head to the side so he could kiss her even deeper. As his tongue slid against hers, he realized how stupid he'd been before. How selfish.

She'd needed him before, needed his strength and he'd refused her.

He wouldn't refuse her again. She could have everything.

Sliding her hands into his hair, she held tightly to him, as if she was afraid he'd back away again. He wasn't going anywhere without her.

Their tongues tangled and she moaned into his mouth, giving him what he wanted, what he'd been craving.

She tasted so damn sweet, he wanted to lick her everywhere. And he would. He and Den would take turns. But for now, there was more than enough of her to go around. Kissing her even harder, he moved his hands to her shoulders, running his palms over her soft skin, feeling the delicate bones beneath. She was curvy and her personality was so big, the fact that she was so delicate hit him like a smack upside the head.

He and Den were big guys. He didn't want to hurt her. And the things he wanted to do to her weren't sweet or pretty. They were dirty and rough. He'd learned to submerge those baser instincts with all of the women he'd been with before.

He didn't want to hide them from her. He felt like she'd take him no matter what. And that was freeing. When she bit his lip, making him groan, he had to wonder if she'd caught a hint of what he was feeling.

Well, no shit, asshole. She's an empathic goddess.

The fact that she didn't turn him away brought all those darker desires closer to the surface.

He let her nip at his tongue before sucking on it and soothing that tiny hurt before he pulled away, staring into her eyes for several seconds. She was breathing hot and heavy, and so was he. She'd sucked her bottom lip between her teeth and was biting on it, the sight making him want to bite her all over.

Then her eyes closed as her body arched and the look on her face was pure sensual pleasure. He needed to see what Den was doing to put that look on her face. Turning, he found Den with his hands on her thighs, pressing them apart while he blew on the dark patch of hair on her mound.

The sound she made when Den moved his hands up her

thighs to shove them under her ass and lift her caused Jacoby's cock to respond with a jerk. *Vaffanculo*, if he wasn't careful, he'd come in his damn pants. And that would be a damn tragedy. He was either coming in her mouth or her pussy.

When Den put his mouth over her pussy and feasted, he couldn't look away. He never would've guessed that his friend was a master at eating out women. Then again, it wasn't like they'd ever shared sex stories. They'd been so damn focused on finding a way out that their plans for escape had consumed them.

Right now, the only thing that mattered was giving her pleasure.

Den used his mouth to suck on her pussy lips for several long seconds before he drew back and played the tip of his tongue over her clit. Her upper body lifted off the bed and Den used his hands to hold her hips down and drive her wild.

"Jack, hold her down."

Jacoby didn't hesitate to follow Den's instructions. Not when he could see how much pleasure she got from Den's mouth.

Sliding up the bed, he settled himself above her, his legs on either side of her body. Drawing her head onto his left thigh, he fastened his hands to her breasts and squeezed.

"Oh, my stars."

She sounded out of breath and completely consumed by desire, her body writhing beneath their hands like a flame, uncontrollable and red-hot. Her skin held a rosy glow it hadn't before, her nipples cherry-red and too damn tempting.

Den's hands looked huge on her hips, holding her tight enough to leave marks. Shifting his gaze, Jacoby saw his own hands left faint impressions where he held her.

That shouldn't make him feel so damn possessive. It did. Hell, it inflamed his desire to own her.

Bending over her, he sealed their mouths together again, the upside-down position giving him a challenge he was more than happy to meet. It forced him to concentrate, to be more controlled.

She met his kiss with a red-hot response, giving back even more. Her lips moved against his as she moaned into his mouth, making his own hunger rush closer to the surface.

He felt her hands curl around his neck, each finger a brand against his skin before she slid them into his hair and brought him even closer, holding him tight. As if she thought he might try to get away.

He was going nowhere, at least not until they'd finished what they'd started.

His hands slid from her shoulders to her breasts, the softness of her skin a taunt. He wanted to feel her breasts against his chest as he fucked her. The image shoved out every last rational thought he might've had. Now, his only mission in life was to make her scream.

Forcing himself to give up her mouth, he shifted his attention to her breasts. In his peripheral vision, he saw Den glance up from between her legs, watching him. Only minutes ago, that might've freaked him out. Now, it barely registered.

She'd become his entire focus.

Pulling her closer, he draped her over his thigh so he could get to her breasts easier. And then he let himself feast. He used his teeth and tongue to torment her, making her squirm as Den continued to hold her down. Den abandoned his own actions for the moment to watch Jacoby.

Sucking on one nipple, he squeezed the other between his thumb and forefinger, plucking at the tip. The sounds she made gave him the most intense satisfaction. As if she were praising him. He wanted nothing more than to make her happy.

Sucking her nipple into his mouth, he tormented her with

bites and licks. He'd never made love to a woman who inspired him to pleasure her more thoroughly than Kari did. And it wasn't simply the fact that she was a goddess, though that might have had a little something to do with it.

Mostly, though, it was simply *her*. She made him want to break her down and hear her cry out his name.

From the corner of his eye, he saw Den return to making love to her pussy with his mouth. And now, she melted. She went boneless in his arms and he knew she was theirs. The frantic urge to own her reared up again and he squeezed her a little bit tighter, bit her a little harder. She responded with sighs that made him want to beat his chest. And demand even more.

But she nearly derailed him when she reached between his legs and cupped his aching cock in her hands.

"Jacoby, I want to suck you while Den fucks me."

Holy hell. Every nerve ending in his body responded like she'd doused him in gasoline and lit a match. The image in his head caused all the breath to leave his lungs, which he quickly sucked back in.

Lifting his head, he caught and held her gaze and...

Holy shit. Were her eyes glowing?

"Jacoby?"

He blinked and shook his head and now the glow was gone. He wondered if it had ever really been there or if he'd imagined it.

Either way, it wouldn't have mattered. He was too far gone.

"Whatever you want, my lady."

She smiled, as if she knew he hadn't meant to use that title to keep her at a distance. No, it was an endearment, one he planned to use a hell of a lot more if it put that smile on her face.

"I want you." Her gaze bored directly into his before sliding to Den. "And I want you. I've been waiting for three months. I don't want to wait any longer."

He completely understood.

Not bothering to check with Den, he laid her back on the bed then rose up on his knees. At the foot of the bed, Den did the same. The sound of two zippers releasing filled the silence that had fallen between them.

A sense of urgency made Jacoby work faster, shoving his pants and underwear down and over his hips. His stiff cock released, jutting forward, as if reaching for her mouth.

The bed shook as Den repositioned himself, spreading her legs even farther. Jacoby watched Den's big hands grip her thighs high on the inside, making her suck in a deep breath.

When he slid them under her thighs and lifted her pelvis up, her teeth sank into her bottom lip. Jacoby switched between watching her and watching Den, letting his own arousal feed off hers.

He saw Den take his thick cock in hand and point it toward her opening. Jacoby had seen Den naked, of course. For the past three months, they'd lived together in a tiny cabin, but Jacoby had never studied the guy's dick before.

Now he couldn't look away. Maybe he was a voyeur. He'd just never had the chance to experience it before. He was pretty sure he was going to like it.

He definitely liked the way Kari responded. He loved watching her eyes shut as Den touched the tip to the lips of her sex and pause there.

"I want you to watch me. Open your eyes, Kari."

Her eyes fluttered open after a few, long seconds then she stared back down at Den. But she reached for Jacoby with her right hand, wrapping it around his exposed cock and beginning a slow pump.

Groaning, Jacoby forced his eyes to remain open so he could watch Den pull her forward, inch by inch, onto his erection.

Her sharp inhale made Den pause for a minute, but she shook her head.

"Don't stop. Feels so good."

Hell, yes, it did. Because the farther Den pushed inside her, the harder she pumped him. And that felt fucking amazing.

You wouldn't think her small hand could grip as tight as she did. *Vaffanculo*, he had to be careful or she'd make him come before he ever got in her mouth. And damn it, he did not want to miss that sensation.

Den set a slow pace at first, his hips pumping forward at an agonizing pace, making Kari's eyes close again and her head drop back onto the bed. But every time he sank all the way to his balls, his next retreat was a little faster, a little less complete. The bed began to shudder beneath the power of Den's thrusts and Kari's continued to stroke to the same rhythm.

If all she did was get him off with her hand, he'd be happy with that. He wouldn't care if she never took him in her mouth. But just as he thought that, she turned her head and tugged him closer, meeting his gaze.

He knew what she wanted.

Sliding one hand behind her head, he lifted her toward him and eased his hips closer until she could put her lips around the head of his cock.

He couldn't contain his groan, which sounded more like a growl as she eased her mouth down the shaft, wetting him with her tongue. The suction of her lips around the head made his hips jerk forward until he'd nearly buried the entire length in her throat.

Fuck. He didn't want to choke her. He tried to pull away, but she stopped him with a hand on his hip. Her gaze linked with his and he had to stomp on the urge to come right then.

The heat in her eyes engorged his cock even more and then she started to work him in earnest.

His head tipped back, and his eyes closed as he let her have whatever she wanted. Her head rested on his thigh with a gentle weight, but the suction of her mouth was powerful. He felt her urge him toward orgasm with every passing second, as if she wanted to make him surrender before she did.

No fucking way. He'd come when she did. If he could hold out that long.

Den was doing everything he could to get her there, but she was fighting him, too. Opening his eyes, Jacoby looked down at her, saw the blissed look on her face and knew it was over.

His cock jerked against her tongue, his balls tightening before he groaned and spilled down her throat.

Groaning, he forced himself to hold still as she continued to suck him then moan around him as she shuddered. The sound she made intensified his orgasm. She'd reached her peak, as well, taking Den along with her, groaning out his release and making the bed shake one last time.

Jacoby could barely breathe, his brain buzzing with white noise, his muscles shaking...and addicted to a goddess who would probably get them all killed.

Not the worst way to go.

SEVEN

Settled into the back seat of the car they'd stolen, Kari floated on a rush of power so intense, she thought she might actually pass out from it.

She hadn't felt power like this for decades. Possibly centuries. Was it because she hadn't had sex like that since possibly the Middle Ages? Or did it have something to do with the two men sitting silent in the front seat? She had a sneaking suspicion it was completely due to those two men.

And that was going to be a problem because, well, they didn't seem at all happy with her. But not even their scowls could make a dent in the peaceful bliss enfolding her.

Sighing, she smiled and caught sight of Den, who was driving at the moment, check her out in the rearview.

His gaze narrowed, probably because of the huge smile on her face, which she refused to temper. When his cheeks flushed a dull red, her smile widened.

"Is everything okay?"

Den's low, husky voice filled the empty spaces in the car with a warmth that made her want to wrap herself around that big body of his and soak in all his strength. Between them, he and Jacoby created enough energy to fill her reserves of power to bursting.

But she knew they were still processing what had happened, so she tried to tone down her smile and not appear completely punch-drunk.

"I'm fine, thank you."

She wanted so badly to ask the same of them but had the sudden fear she'd regret it. Then again, she was an honest-to-goodness goddess, a deity of the Etruscan pantheon, and she didn't do regrets.

"I guess the bigger question is," she paused and watched both men's shoulders tense, "how are you?"

Den shot a look at Jacoby, who continued to stare straight ahead. Silence held for a few long seconds before one of them answered it just wasn't the one she'd expected.

"We're fine." Jacoby turned his head to look over the seat at her, his gaze direct. "You don't have anything to worry about."

Yeah, she wasn't buying that. "I think we need to talk about what happened last night."

Now Den and Jacoby did exchange glances. And they apparently came to the same conclusion.

"Fine. Let's talk."

Her mouth dropped open at Jacoby's calm statement. Her mouth dropped open, but words escaped her for several moments. Obviously, she'd completely misread them.

"First, tell us how you're feeling."

Huh? "I feel fine." She frowned. "Wait, are you feeling okay?"

Scooting forward until she could reach over the seats, she put her hands on their shoulders. She didn't sense any weakness in either of them, allaying the fear that she'd drained them last night. But she did sense a darker tinge to their emotions this morning.

Twisting in his seat, Jacoby looked straight at her.

"We're fine." He slid a quick glance at Den, whose hands curled around the steering wheel just a little tighter. "We're actually better than fine. Both of us feel...energized. Strong. We figure that has something to do with you, but we need you to tell us that for certain."

Her gaze narrowed as she sensed an undercurrent in Jacoby's tone and felt his worry. Not fear. He wasn't afraid. But he was definitely worried.

"Sex, especially good sex, creates powerful magic. It recharged my powers and I assume it did the same for both of you. Don't the *Mal* use sex magic?"

It would surprise her if they didn't. From what she knew about the *Mal*, they used any means necessary to gain power.

"Yes." Den answered this time, after a quick glance in the mirror. "I've just never done it."

"Neither have I," Jacoby added. "We just wanted to be sure something else wasn't going on that we needed to know about."

"Is something else going on?"

Jacoby paused again, as if carefully considering his response. "My ability to manipulate metal seems to have magnified exponentially after having sex with you. And Den's power has increased, too."

Well, now. That was interesting. "I've never heard of the power transfer going both ways with deities." She answered truthfully, not wanting to hide anything from them. "Typically, the men who share their energy with a deity feel drained, not energized."

She'd been so focused on her own powers she hadn't taken the time to check theirs. She'd been concerned that she'd drained them but hadn't thought that they'd be anything other than normal.

She should've known better. These two men were nothing if

not extraordinary. There had to be a reason they'd been sent into her life.

Her sister, Nortia, Goddess of Fate, could be a straight-up bitch at times but she was still a compassionate person at her core. If she had been fated to meet Jacoby and Den, maybe Nortia had had a hand in arranging that. Which meant maybe she needed to have a discussion with her sister. And she would, when she got back to civilization. Right now, she needed to keep Den and Jacoby from thinking they were somehow anything other than perfect for her.

Closing her eyes, she let her empathy reach out for them, let her power caress theirs.

What she found shocked the hell out of her. Their power *had* grown stronger. So much so, they were bleeding power. Anyone with a magical gift would get a charge just from being in their vicinity. She'd never seen anything like it. It was almost like they were feeding each other power in an endless loop.

"Do you two feel that?"

Her eyes opened wide, looking at each of them in turn and watching the way they glanced at each other.

"Yes," Jacoby said. "We've never had a connection like this before. We're concerned it'll make it easier for whoever's following to find us. And you."

She wanted to sniffle. They were still worried about her. It was so sweet, she wanted to crawl into the front seat and kiss them both. Which might cause an accident and therefore was ill-advised.

Still...

"I don't think we have to worry about that. And once we get to the den, the wards will mask you from anyone looking for you. We just need to get to the den."

"We should be there within the hour," Den said. "And then

we need to figure out how the hell we're going to get the fuck out away from the *Mal* without getting killed."

HALF AN HOUR LATER, Den turned onto an unmarked lane somewhere in southeastern Pennsylvania. The terrain was hilly and thickly forested. If Kari hadn't told him exactly where to turn, he would've missed it completely.

To the naked eye, the path looked like little more than a break in the trees but once he turned, the path opened into a black-topped road.

Damn, the wards that kept this place disguised from the rest of the world were strong.

"How many acres do they own?"

"I don't know." Kari shrugged, looking out the window into the trees. She'd been quiet since their earlier discussion about the increase in his and Jacoby's powers. She didn't look worried but she seemed to perk up once they entered *lucani* lands. "A hundred acres. More, probably. They bought the original land over a hundred years ago and I know they've added to it through the years."

Holy shit. The amount of power needed to maintain the wards on an area this size had to be immense.

"The *Mal* like to say the *lucani* are an unorganized group of inbreds and rednecks. That they're no better than the animals they shift into."

Jacoby's quiet statement drew Den's attention away from the twisty road for a few seconds. Jacoby's expression didn't show much but Den heard his controlled anger in his voice. Or maybe Den was simply seeing his own emotions in Jacoby. Whatever the case, they were both pissed off and ready to rip someone's head off. And that was probably a mistake when they were about to meet the entire *lucani* den.

"I'm sure they told you a lot of things you know aren't true."

Den checked the rearview to see Kari watching Jacoby, worry written plainly on her face.

She had every right to be worried. The *lucani* might take one look at them and decide he and Jacoby were too much of a risk and kill them both. They'd be totally outnumbered and Den was fairly certain if it came to a battle of strength, they'd be overwhelmed, even if they used their powers to defend themselves.

Den felt the power emanating from the land. Jacoby wasn't the only one who'd seen an increase in power. Den's Goddess gift had never been useful as a weapon. His affinity to animals extended only far enough to enable him to understand what they were thinking or feeling. He couldn't talk to them or control them. He didn't want to. He had more respect for other living creatures than to bend them to his will.

Of course, if he'd been more powerful, the *Mal* would've forced him to use his power against their enemies. And if he'd been born *Mal* instead of simply being born into a *Mal* family, he probably would've learned how to hone that ability during his soldier training.

Now... He'd defend himself against the only family he had to keep from using another living being against their will. He also knew he'd do whatever was necessary to make sure Kari was safe. And if that meant killing anyone who dared hurt her, so be it.

His hands tightened around the steering wheel as he saw the first home to the left of the road. He only caught a glimpse as it was carefully surrounded by trees, but now he felt like he was being watched. That feeling intensified as they began to see more homes.

If an *eteri* somehow managed to find their way onto *lucani* property through the wards that would try to direct them away, they'd find an average-looking community of homes. All were constructed of stone and wood, most of them only one story tall.

None looked run down or in need of repair. Some had gardens, though they weren't perfectly manicured like most of the *Mal*-owned houses. No, these were wild and filled with birds and insects. Not surprisingly, he didn't sense a lot of small animals. The fact that wolves roamed here probably kept them away.

Finally, the road led them to a group of buildings that probably classified as a village. Only one of them had a second story and that was probably their destination. The ten men and five women standing on the porch confirmed his assumption. Especially when one of those women turned out to be his mother.

Relief, pure and fierce swept through his body with the force of a gale.

Slamming the car into park, he got out and headed straight for her as she rushed off the porch. No one attempted to stop her and that was probably a really good thing because he wasn't sure he would've been able to stop himself from hurting people if they had.

Christ, she must be terrified.

"Mom."

"Denny, sweetheart. You're okay. I've been so worried."

As she wrapped her thin arms around his neck and hugged him tight, he returned her affection, just made sure not to grip her too tightly. She'd been ill for so long, he'd learned at an early age to be gentle with her.

"Are you okay? You aren't hurt?"

Pulling away, he set his hands on her shoulders and set her away from him so he could check her out from head to foot. She looked fine. Especially when she lifted her eyebrows and gave him a Mom glare.

"Of course, I'm fine. I mean, it would've been nice to have a heads up that two strange men were going to show up at my home and ask me to run away with them. If I'd been a little younger, I might've embarrassed myself by thinking they were there for purposes other than kidnapping. But I guess I'm too old for that sort of thing now."

Den had no idea what to say to that. His mom had never been one to make jokes, especially not around his father. He knew their marriage had been one of convenience, which is why most *Mal* got married. But he'd never heard her say anything as innuendo-filled as that statement.

"Mom? Did you hit your head?"

At least her laughter sounded the same. "Yes, sweetheart, I'm fine. But I've been worried about you. The *lucani* have tried to fill me on what's been going on, but I don't think they know all the facts, either, do they?"

"No, we don't. And we'd really love to hear all about it."

The man standing at the top of the porch with his arms crossed over his chest stared at Den with steady eyes. Dressed in suit pants and a white dress shirt, his feet bare, he walked down the stairs.

Den thought the man would stop in front of him and demand an explanation. Instead, he walked right by him, straight to Kari, who wore a wide smile.

"Lady Kari." The guy executed a perfect bow, which made Den's mouth drop open a split second before every atom in his body rose up in fury. If he touched her, Den would break his hand. "Are you okay?"

She reached for his arm, drawing him up so she could wrap her arms around his shoulders and give him a hug. Luckily, she initiated the embrace or Den would've ripped the guy's head off his shoulders. A quick glance at Jacoby and he knew he would've done the same.

"Cole, it's so good to see you. You look tired. You're not getting enough sleep, are you? I've told you, you can't run on coffee and adrenaline all the time. You need downtime."

So this was the *lucani* king. He'd seen pictures, of course. All *Mal* enforcers knew that if they ever came upon the king undefended, they were to shoot him on sight. Den had always wondered why the *Mal* were so frightened of him.

Standing beside him, Den understood a little better why the *Mal* feared him so much. He didn't look particularly fierce but, damn, the man had presence. An air of total command that you didn't get from simply having power. No, this was something you earned and built over years. A force of will that made good leaders great.

And the guy was barely thirty.

"Yes, Lady. I'd love to have some downtime if certain goddesses would stop getting in trouble."

Kari laughed and the sound struck a chord deep inside of Den, one that rang only for her.

"Well, with the help of two wonderful men, I'm free again."

"And voted most likely to get in trouble," a female voice sounded behind them. "Tinia's teat, Kari, why were you gone so long?"

Den glanced over his shoulder at the woman rushing out of the woods, flanked by two men. A woman who looked almost exactly like Kari.

Den's mouth dropped open as the women embraced.

"I'm pretty sure you know exactly why I was gone for so long, but I am sorry I scared you, Ami."

Sisters. This was Munthukh, Lady Amity.

"Why don't we let the ladies get caught up—"

"My sister. She's not here."

Shit. Den automatically searched the small crowd for the familiar face of Jacoby's sister, Emelia, and realized she wasn't here.

He'd been so damn happy to see his mom he hadn't even looked for her.

"No." Cole faced Jacoby, arms over his chest. "We weren't able to get to her. The *Mal* had already moved her."

The look on Jacoby's face made Den's chest ache. Damn it. Just...

"I need to go after her."

Cole held up one hand and Den drew himself a little straighter. If he told Jacoby he couldn't go, they were about to have a fight on their hands.

"Jacoby, right? I'm Cole Luporeale. I understand you're anxious to get to your sister and you have my word we will. We just need a little more information. Why don't you and Den," Cole glanced at him with a nod, "come inside and we can talk?"

Talk? More like be subdued and contained and taken out of the equation. Den had no doubt that whatever happened now, he and Jacoby were about to be put out of the picture.

Isn't that what you expected all along?

Yeah, he had. Jacoby, too. They just hadn't discussed what they would do when they go to this point. He'd kind of figured they'd fight until they no longer could and then they'd do whatever the *lucani* wanted so their loved ones would be safe.

They hadn't expected to want to stay by the side of their woman. And no matter that she was a goddess, Kari was theirs. Or more to the point, they were hers.

They'd fight to stay by her side. But now that she was free, would she want to stay with them?

JACOBY HAD KNOWN the second he hadn't seen Emelia on the porch that he had to go back out and get her. And he'd fight every single *lucani* in the area to do it.

"My father probably heard about Den's mother and moved Emelia. I need to leave immediately."

"I understand your concern." The *lucani* king looked him straight in the eyes. "But you're going to need our help if you want to get her out. That's all we're offering. Help. She's your sister. We don't want to get in the way."

"And you're just going to let us walk away?"

"If that's what you want, yes. But we're more than willing to give you whatever assistance you think you're going to need. I have four *sicari* and our tracker ready to move out immediately. They're more than capable but if you think you need more men, I can have another five available."

Sicari? Jacoby had the vague knowledge that the word meant assassin. His gaze skipped to the remaining men standing on the porch. Yeah, they certainly looked the part of assassins. They stared at him as if they were dissecting, checking out his weaknesses.

He had two at the moment. He shot Den a glance and knew his friend had his back, no matter what he decided.

"So you can put my sister in another cage? She's been in one all her life. I don't want to get her out just to have her trapped again."

"You have my word that won't happen. But you don't need to take only my word."

Turning, he held his hand out to the young redhead standing next to one of the men on the porch. She couldn't be more than twenty, but she looked...old. Not physically but there was something in her eyes.

She shared a quick glance with the man at her side and Jacoby saw a resemblance. Family. Maybe father and daughter. The guy definitely felt protective about her, whoever she was.

As she came closer, he felt the power emanating from her. He didn't recognize her, but he did realize a second before she stopped in front of him what she was.

Holy shit.

His expression must have shown his thoughts because her lips curved in a wry smile.

"Hi, I'm Cat. I'm so sorry about your sister, but I give you my word, as the..." her pause was infinitesimal but unmistakable, "Goddess of the Moon, she will be in total control of every decision. Please, we just want to help."

Well, shit. He didn't know what to say. He didn't know if he should bow or kiss her ring, not that she was wearing a ring.

He settled for bowing his head. "Thank you, Lady Cat. I didn't mean to offend anyone. I'm just worried."

Walking forward, Cat reached for his arm and squeezed, smiling up at him. "I get it. Please, let me introduce you to my dad. He's one of the *sicari* Cole was talking about. You can trust him."

When she spoke, he believed every word. Which was a strange feeling for a man who'd learned not to trust anyone except Den and his sister.

"Then I'll be happy to talk to him, Lady."

Her grimace was adorable. "Please, call me Cat." She leaned in closer so only he could hear her. "Lady makes me feel old."

He smiled for the first time in what felt like years. "Whatever you want, Cat."

Her answering smile shone bright. "I know you want to get moving so..." She turned and nodded at the men on the porch, none of whom looked thrilled to see him so close to her. He didn't have time to worry about that now.

The man who looked to be Cat's dad came down off the

porch. When he got close enough, he held out his hand. Jacoby shook it. The man didn't grip him too hard or try to exert his dominance in any other way. He just shook, the tats on his arms stark on his skin. Jacoby thought he recognized them as protective runes.

"Kyle Rossini." He gestured behind him at the remaining people on the porch. "My team and I are ready to give you whatever support you need. We just need you to lead the way."

FIVE MINUTES LATER, Jacoby, Den, Cole, Kyle, the three other *sicari* and the tracker, Kaisie, sat at a table in the two-story building, staring at a map of New Jersey.

"They're going to take her to this safe house outside of Millville." He pointed at the tiny dot on map. "It's the most defensible and the most heavily warded of the properties my father owns."

"Why do you think they'll take here there and not to one of the *Mal*'s strongholds?" The female *sicari* Kaine asked. "Does your dad have enough power in the organization to dictate a move like this?"

Jacoby nodded. "Yeah, he does. My father's high enough on the food chain he was able to get me on the detail to guard Kari. Everything with him is image. In the *Mal*, if you look powerful, that's half the battle. Besides, he was born *Malandante*. He wasn't just born into a *Mal* family. Plus, he's powerful enough on his own to have risen up the ranks anyway."

"What about you?" Kaine tilted her head up and looked at him. "How powerful are you?"

He felt Den watching him intently and lifted his head to meet his gaze. What he saw there convinced him to continue.

He directed his response to Cole. "My parents believe my

powers are pretty much worthless. What they don't know is that they've been strengthening for years. I've managed to keep that mostly to myself. Den and Emelia know. And in the past couple of weeks," his jaw clenched as he tried not to embarrass himself by getting a hard on when he thought about what they'd done with Kari, "they've increased exponentially."

No one said anything, probably because Cole didn't respond. He just moved on.

"What can you do to help, besides fight?"

"I can manipulate metal."

Cole didn't look surprised at his revelation. "So you're an *armifictor*?"

Jacoby shook his head. "I don't know what that is."

Cole's brows rose before he could control his response. "A weapons maker. You've never heard the term before?"

"No."

"And the *Mal* don't know what you can do?"

He shook his head again.

"Then that's something we can take advantage of." Cole looked at Den. "You have any tricks up your sleeve we should know about?"

"I've got a minor Goddess Gift. Nothing weaponizable."

"And you don't want to share with the rest of the class?" Kaine's tone held humor and more than a little goading.

Den looked her straight in the eyes. "I've got an affinity for animals. I can understand them. Sometimes I can even encourage them to do things for me."

"Then there's someone you're going to want to meet while you're here." Cole pointed back at the map. "But first, let's concentrate on getting Jacoby's sister. If you're sure this is where they're going to take her, we need a detailed map and we need a game plan fast. We need to get this done tonight, before they have time to settle in."

The only other woman in the room, who hadn't spoken and hadn't introduced herself, grabbed a pen and a pad off the desk across the room and slid it across the table to Jacoby. He took both but hesitated for a few long seconds.

He did this and he gave up any chance of reconciliation with his parents. And even though he and Emelia had talked about defecting in general terms before, she'd never said she absolutely wanted to be free.

What if she didn't want to leave? What if she didn't want to take the mantle of Kari's power? What if Kari didn't want to give up her powers?

"Jack?"

Den's voice made him look up and when their gazes caught and held, Den nodded.

"She wants out. Don't second guess everything now. This is the right thing to do."

He took a deep breath. And started sketching.

BY MID-AFTERNOON, more than two hours after they'd arrived, Kari was ready to march into the office in the common hall and haul Den and Jacoby out of there. She knew they were planning their mission to get Jacoby's sister and she knew that was important, but she hated not knowing what was going on.

True, she could just walk in and ask what was going on. It wasn't like they'd forbidden her to enter or deliberately not invited her to the meeting of the minds.

She'd made the decision to stay with Amity and have a little much-needed sister time. Which had turned into more than she'd bargained for when Lucy and Nortia had shown up. Of course, they'd wanted to know all about her men, about whom she'd been happy to tell.

But after an hour, she'd started looking at the clock. Would they leave without her?

Nortia's loud sigh caught her attention and Kari's head whipped around to stare at her.

"What?"

"Do you really have to ask me what I'm thinking?" Nortia rolled sky-blue eyes, which made Kari want to stick her tongue out at her sister. "Seriously, you're smarter than that."

No, she didn't have to ask. She knew exactly what Nortia had on her mind. The wry look on her face gave it away.

"You're pining. It's not attractive."

Lucy and Amity grinned. Kari glared at them, but she couldn't hold it long. She wasn't mad at them. She was worried.

And maybe it was time to start doing something rather than worry.

"Is it weird when you talk to Lia, knowing who she is?" She directed her question at Nortia, who rolled her eyes again and kept silent. "I know you haven't told her yet and I understand why but...does it make things awkward between you? Could you feel a connection when you talked? Lucy, you knew Cat for years. Did knowing she was your replacement change the way you felt about her?"

Lucy rolled with the change in the direction of the conversation pretty well.

"I'm ashamed to say I wasn't as accepting as I could have been at first. She picked up on that pretty quickly, which made me feel pretty shitty."

When she turned to Nortia, she considered herself lucky her sister didn't tell her to fuck off, which would be a very Nortia thing to do. Instead, she thought about it for a second.

"Yes, it's strange. But Lia's still too younger and it's going to be a few years until she's strong enough to take over the mantle. I have a little time to figure out how I'm going to tell her. Did you say Jacoby's sister already knows? Do you know how she knows?"

"I don't have any idea."

"I do."

The voice came from the other side of the room, where a pale figure slowly materialized.

"Tilly!" Calling out her name, Kari ran across the floor and threw her arms around the elusive Goddess of the Spirit. An underworld goddess who rarely left her post in Aitás, Hinthial returned her hug, another surprise.

"Hello, Kari. It's good to see you." Her gaze skipped around the room. "And all of you."

"How did you sneak away from Charun?"

A small smile from a goddess who very rarely did. "He's been otherwise occupied lately."

"How's Perry?" Amity asked.

Which begged Kari's question, "Who's Perry?"

Amity's eyes widened. "Oh, I forgot. You totally missed that. Long story short. Perry was a patient of mine. Burn victim. Charun fell for her and she went to live with him in Aitás."

Kari's mouth dropped open. "Say what now?"

"Right?" Nortia help up one hand. "Shocked the hell out of me, too."

"And your men are Cat's guardians." Kari pointed at Amity. "And your man is still half goat." She turned to Hinthial, who rolled her eyes. Then she turned to Nortia. "And your man... Wait, you don't have a man, unless I missed something in the months I was gone."

"Would you like me to entwine your fate with that of a steer in cattle country?" Nortia spoke so sweetly, Kari had to laugh. "I'm perfectly content on my own. Much easier that way. Most men aren't worth the trouble."

"You used to say no man was worth the trouble." Amity

focused her full attention on Nortia now. "I wonder what changed."

"Nothing's changed for me but you all seem to have found men who make you happy so there must be some decent men in the world."

"Oh, there are. Most definitely."

All eyes turned back to Kari.

"So I was right." Amity crossed her arms over her chest, her lips curved in a knowing smile. "There is something going on with the three of you."

"What is it with you both having two men?" Lucy shook her head. "I have my hands full with just one."

Kari exchanged a smile with Amity, whose expression lightened.

"Don't knock it 'til you try it." Kari sighed. "And speaking of my two men, I think I need to go find them. I know they're planning to go get Jacoby's sister and I have the feeling I need to go with them."

"Do you really think that's necessary?" Amity leaned forward and took her hand. "You just got away. I don't think you should put yourself that close to the *Mal* again. What if they take you and Jacoby's sister? That would be a catastrophe."

"I need to be there for her. I just know I do."

Amity gave a long sigh. "Then let's hope your men are as good as you think they are. I don't want to lose you again."

"Trust me, I don't want to be lost. But I also don't want to sit on the sidelines and be useless anymore. I need to do this."

EIGHT

"This is a really bad idea." Jacoby.

"I wish you'd rethink this." Den.

"Lady Kari, I really think you should stay." Cole. "We have no idea what we're up against and we know they targeted you specifically."

"With all due respect, your highness." Kaine stood next to Kari, arms on her hips, glaring at her king. "You're treating a goddess like she's weak. Chill. Respectfully, sir."

Kari gave the *sicari* Kaine a hug as she watched the *lucani* king grimace and visibly wince. He deserved to be taken down a few pegs, but she needed to have a talk with Den and Jacoby before they left. And they would have that talk in just a few minutes. First, she needed to clear up a few misconceptions among the five men currently hovering around her, trying to make her change her mind and remain here.

Drawing herself up to her full height, which was barely over five-four but still, she stared at each man in turn. All of them had the good sense to let their gazes fall. She might've been a mostly useless goddess for the past several hundred years, but she was still a goddess, not some vapid fake celebrity who thought the world wanted to know her every move.

"So here's how this is going to play out. Cole, you're staying here, since we can't have you too close the *Mal*. If they make another attempt on your life, who's to say they won't get lucky this time? And that would be bad now, wouldn't it?

"I promise to stay out of the way of the operation unless I feel you need help in any way. Then all bets are off. I may not be able to become a wolf but I'm not helpless either. So don't treat me as if I am and we'll all get out of this together. Now, if you don't mind, I'd like to speak to Den and Jacoby for a few minutes. Alone. We'll be ready to leave by six. You can go on and do what needs to be done."

She looked at Jacoby and Den, who did not look away as the others had done. And that made her smile. If they were going to stick around for the next hundred years or so, they needed to be able to stand up to her.

But she couldn't allow them to risk themselves for her while not allowing her to take the same risk. They needed to have this discussion now.

"Cole, is there a more private room where we can talk?"

"Second floor, Lady Kari. At the end on the left."

She gave Cole a smile as she headed out of the room, knowing Jacoby and Den would follow her. She was pretty sure she heard either Kaisie or Kyle mutter "Good luck" to her men as they followed behind her. Nice to know she still had the ability to make males nervous.

No one said anything as they climbed the stairs to the second floor and made their way to the room, which turned out to be a bedroom. So that's why Cole had been smiling as she left. She might have to revise her opinion of the *lucani* king as needing to get a clue. Maybe he had more of a clue than she gave him credit for.

Walking across the room, she stood on the opposite side of the bed then crossed her arms over her chest and stared at her men. Both of them stared back, their determination clear in the flat lines of their mouths.

"You need to stay here." Den surprised her by starting. She'd thought for sure it'd be Jacoby. "Far away from the *Mal*."

"And you both need to understand that I'm coming with you. I didn't bring you up here to rehash his. I only wanted you to know—"

Jacoby wrapped one arm around her shoulders and the other around her hip and lifted her off the floor until their lips were level. And then he kissed her. Hard. He stole every ounce of breath in her body and lit the fire that'd been banked since they'd arrived here.

He kissed her hard enough that her lips parted from the pressure. Not that she wouldn't have opened to him, but he didn't give her the chance. He took the advantage and slipped his tongue between her lips, tangling with her tongue in a kiss that went from hot to incendiary in the space of a few seconds.

She tasted his fear for her on his lips, but she also sensed a deeper need and she understood that. She welcomed it. And she let him have what he needed. Which apparently was her.

He attacked her mouth with single-minded focus, let him lace his fingers through her hair and pull her head back so his mouth could travel down her neck. Her pussy clenched on a wave of desire so strong, she cried out as her hands slid beneath the collar of his shirt so she could touch his bare skin.

As if her touch ignited even more sparks, Jacoby moved his hands to her hips—and held her away from him.

She was about to complain but Den was there to take her, wrapping his arms around her waist and holding her against his hard chest, his erect cock pressing into the cleft of her ass, igniting another round of sparks in her blood that threatened to make her a creature of pure sensation.

And when Jacoby's hands went straight for the zipper of his pants, her gaze dropped to watch as he shoved them down just far enough to release his cock.

"This isn't going to be slow and easy."

Her smile made the heat in his eyes smolder.

"I'm easy enough."

"But only for us," Den growled in her ear.

"I'm pretty sure I can live with that. But only if you both fuck me right now."

"That's the plan." Jacoby looked over his shoulder. "On the bed."

Again, Kari silently blessed Cole for sending them to this room, which had a king-size bed. Apparently the *lucani* king was a mind reader.

Den didn't waste any time. He walked her straight to the bed and set her down on her knees on the mattress. She quickly turned to find both men tearing their clothes off, staring at her with lust plain on their faces. Jacoby had had a head start on Den and now stood naked in front of her.

"This is how crazy you make me," Jacoby said. "There's no way in hell we should be doing this now. And there's no way in hell I'm stopping now."

"I don't want you to stop." She smiled at them. "Besides, think how powerful you'll be afterward. Think of it as juicing before the big game."

Jacoby's lips parted as if he'd been going to say something. Then threw his head back and laughed. She knew he'd never laughed like that in her presence before and it made her smile to hear it. Behind him, Den shook his head as he drew his shirt over it.

"Then I'm more than happy to help the cause. You two go ahead and get started. I'll be back in a second."

Den turned and headed for the door on the far wall, which she assumed was a bathroom, but her gaze flew back to Jacoby as he came closer. His lips still curved in a smile as he stopped inches from the bed. If she reached out, she could take his cock in her hand and stroke him. Instead, she lay back, spread her legs, and crooked a finger at him.

"Come here and show me how much you want me."

"Can't you tell?"

It was her turn to smile. "I can see. I want to feel."

He didn't waste another second. He covered her with his body and sealed his mouth against hers, kissing her with a passion flavored with a deeper emotion she'd yet to give a name. The time for that would come later.

Right now... Well, she wanted to come.

Wrapping her arms around his shoulders, she felt his thighs brush against the inside of hers, felt the head of his cock press against her labia, spreading them open and lodging at her entrance. The ache in her gut spread through the rest of her body but particularly to her sex, which practically begged to be filled.

Gasping, she stared up at him as he pulled his lips away.

"Jacoby, come inside," she begged. "Please."

"I will. I need to. I just want to take," he pressed in another half inch, "it," and another, "slow."

"I don't think I can take slow. Fuck me hard and fast."

His gaze burned into hers. "No way in hell."

He thrust inside her in increments designed to make her crazy. Her body writhed beneath his, tempting him to go faster. Her legs wrapped around his waist, her heels urging him to speed up.

But he had much more control than she'd realized. He set a

pace that drew her out of herself and into a state where she could barely catch her breath. Every sensation was heightened, and she became a creature of pure pleasure.

She barely realized that Den had returned until the bed dipped to the side. Jacoby rolled them until she was now on top but if she thought she was going to get more control, she was sorely mistaken.

She never saw Den, but she felt his hands on her hips, felt Jacoby press her hips down to meet his, lodging his cock deep inside her body. Then she felt Den's slick fingers at her rear entrance. He pushed his fingers inside slowly as she moaned.

She was no stranger to double penetration, but it had been a while. She'd forgotten how damn good it felt. She heard the men say something to each other, but she was too lost in sensation to care. She only wanted to be filled, to be taken and pushed over that edge of pain and pleasure. By the time Den had positioned his cock, she was panting.

"Do it," she managed to say. "Now."

Jacoby began to pull out as Den pushed in and, oh my stars, she shuddered from the riot of sensations coursing through her body.

Desire became an ache that ate away at her from the inside out. Two warm male bodies trapped hers between them and she never wanted to be anywhere else.

Her men found the perfect rhythm after a few short seconds, filling her alternately until she could no longer take it, no matter how much she tried to contain herself.

Her climax ripped through her body, a powerful force that lit every atom in her body.

Now, this was power.

NINE

Jacoby drew in a deep breath and swore he could taste the tension in the car.

Before they'd left the den, he and Den had considered tying her to the bed and leaving her there until they returned. Of course, they'd nixed that fast because she would've snapped her fingers and made their balls disappear. Instead, she sat in the seat behind them, staring out the window. She didn't look worried. She looked ready.

Jacoby checked on Den, who had his head turned toward the side window and his hands clenched into fists on his thighs.

In the rearview, he saw the two cars carrying the *lucani* behind them. They'd been on the road for two hours and had nearly reached their target. The closer they got, the more he wanted to stop and beg, plead, order, *force* her to stay behind.

His father would've pulled in every resource to protect Emelia. The bastard had never paid any attention to her until someone farther up the *Mal* food chain had noticed something unusual in her aura. Jacoby still wasn't sure how they'd finally determined who Emelia was meant to be. She'd never told him. He only knew she believed it and he believed in her.

That's when they'd started planning to get out. And when Jacoby had been assigned to guard Kari, he and Den had agreed it was time to put their plan into motion. To get them the hell out of the *Mal*'s hands.

And here they were, possibly putting Kari back into those hands. The thought made him physically ill. In the past three months, she'd become more than a beautiful woman worthy of worship. She'd become the central point in a triangle he hadn't realized he'd wanted to be a part of. And now, he couldn't think of life without it.

"Kari. You have the panic button, yes?"

She'd refused to carry a weapon of any kind. He and Den had argued with her for at least fifteen minutes about carrying a knife, at the very least. She'd lifted an eyebrow at them and reminded them that she was a goddess of health. She didn't take lives. She healed hearts and souls. How the hell was he supposed to respond to that?

They'd realized you didn't. You moved on to fight another battle. To get her to stay at the car. They'd lost that one, too. He would make sure it didn't come to that.

"Yes." She held up her hand and shook the bracelet around her wrist. Lady Amity had given it to her then shown her the matching one around her own wrist. "At the first sign of trouble, I'll be sure to press the button and have you running back to my side to save me."

Okay, yeah, that sounded a little sexist. A lot sexist.

Vaffanculo, just put him in a wifebeater and give him a case of Budweiser.

"Kari—"

Den poked his arm, out of Kari's sight, and Jacoby shut the fuck up.

"Yes, we're Neanderthals," Den said. "And we'll apologize for that as many times as you want...as soon as we're back at the den with Emelia. I will worship you with my mouth and make you come as many times as you want. And Jacoby will let you do whatever you like with his body for as long as you want. As soon as we're back at the den."

Now she was smiling, and Jacoby knew they'd dodged a bullet.

"You certainly do know the way to a girl's heart." Scooting forward on the bench seat in the back of the white Toyota sedan Cole had assigned them for the trip, she put her hands on both of their shoulders. "But the panic button goes both ways. If either of you is in trouble, I expect you to ask for help."

Her touch made Jacoby want to promise her anything she asked for. Except for this. If he had the chance, he'd make sure they never came after Emelia again. And if that meant showing his father exactly what he could do with his power, then he had no problem with making them hurt.

"Jacoby? What's going on?"

Shit. Her worried tone made him realize she must've picked up on his thoughts.

"Nothing. Nothing's wrong."

"Please don't lie to—"

"We're here."

She fell silent as Jacoby made the turn into the unmarked lane about a mile from his father's Jersey estate. He and Kyle, the *lucani*'s head *sicari*, had decided this was the best place to stage before they made their way on foot to the estate. This land belonged to another *Mal* family, but they'd abandoned the house years ago and the last Jacoby knew, it'd begun to deteriorate. No one had been here in years. The rutted lane and encroaching forest helped that theory, and when they finally pulled up to the house, Jacoby knew he was right.

"Wow, how beautiful this must have been years ago."

"As long as I've known about this place, no one has taken care of it or visited."

"Such a shame."

"Not really, considering the *Mal* who lived here kept *lucani* as guard dogs. They enslaved their minds and turned them into beasts."

Kari's hand tightened on his shoulder for a second. "They have a lot to answer for, but let's not forget...our main goal is to get your sister and get back to the den safely."

He knew that. He also knew the second he saw his father, he was going to want to hurt him. Badly.

"I know." He turned to see Den watching him with narrowed eyes. His friend obviously knew him too well.

But Den didn't say anything. When Den nodded at him, he dipped his head in acknowledgment and got out of the car.

———

DEN KNEW Jacoby had a lot of pent-up hatred for his father. It's what had first bonded them. But where Den had simply wanted to save his mother, Jacoby was determined to hurt his father where it would truly count. In his standing in the *Mal*.

And that meant showing just how powerful Jacoby was and how much his father was losing when Jacoby took his sister away from him. Which meant Den needed to be by Jacoby's side the entire time to watch his back. Because Jacoby was going to do something stupid. He just knew it.

Combined with the fact that Kari had refused to stay with her sister at the *lucani* den... Yeah. He already felt his temples tightening with a headache he couldn't afford now. They had to be razor-sharp if this was going to work.

He had no doubt the *lucani* were up to the task. He'd spoken to Kyle and Kaisie and they both had way more experience at this than either Den or Jacoby. They'd always been grunts, never truly part of the upper structure, even though their fathers had been born *Mal*.

From the corner of his eye, he caught sight of the female *sicari* shedding her clothes and deliberately turned his back to her. And kept it that way. Instinctively, he knew it'd be rude to watch unless she'd given him permission, which she hadn't.

He noticed Jacoby had done the same, giving his gun another once-over.

"Hey." He leaned over so only Jacoby could hear him. "Maybe you should stay back here with Kari."

Jacoby gave him a look he couldn't mistake and didn't bother to respond. Yeah, he'd known that wasn't going to go over well.

"Okay then, just don't do anything stupid."

"Define stupid."

"Jack."

Jacoby paused for a second before he looked up. "I'll be fine. I'm not going to do anything stupid. But if something happens to me, make sure you get Emelia out."

Den nodded but didn't have time to add anything because Kyle walked over with Kaisie, three huge wolves at his sides. Damn, they were amazingly beautiful animals. With human eyes.

That kinda freaked him out.

"We're ready to go." Kyle nodded at Jacoby. "Lead the way. Don't worry about Kaine, Duke, and Nic. You won't see them, but they'll be there when you need them. Den, you're bringing up the rear with Kari."

As much as he felt he needed to stay with Jacoby, he also knew neither of them would be able to concentrate if Kari wasn't protected by one of them. So he gripped his gun a little tighter and nodded. Kari stepped up beside him as Kyle went to Jacoby and they headed off into the woods.

A delicate hand squeezed his forearm for a few seconds and he looked down. Kari smiled at him.

"Have a little faith, Den. Sometimes, you need that just as much as you need courage or planning."

He nodded but didn't say anything. He had faith. In her. In Jacoby. Hell, he even had it in the *lucani*, whom he'd just met. But he also knew sometimes things happened that you had no control over.

And that, more than anything, worried the hell out of him.

THEY HAD no trouble getting to the mansion in the heart of the property. The forest that hid the building from the rest of the world provided excellent cover for invaders. That didn't mean there weren't traps. Both physical and magical.

Kyle had a spell to get them through the wards without notice, and then it was up to everyone else to be on the lookout for the physical traps laid throughout the woods. Jacoby knew where they had been laid in years past, but that didn't mean his father hadn't had his security team move them. Luckily for them, and pretty stupidly on the part of his father or his team, he hadn't moved them in twenty years.

They'd decided not to wait until dark to enter. There were usually fewer guards during the day, especially around dinnertime. Maybe his father thought intruders wouldn't be so brazen in the light of day. Whatever the reason, they planned to make it work to their advantage.

When the house came into sight, the *lucani* spread out to check the entry and exit points and count guards. Jacoby, Den, and Kari waited out of sight of the house for Kyle to return. Jacoby had a hard time staying put but having Kari by his side helped.

When Kyle finally melted back out of the trees, he used his fingers to designate how many guards then motioned them to follow.

Four outside. Two inside on the first floor. Three upstairs gathered in one place. That had to be where they were keeping Emelia.

They headed for the rear of the house, where only the kitchen looked out onto the forest from the first floor. At this time of day, the only person in there would be the cook, an older woman who'd been with the family for as long as Jacoby could remember.

The door had a standard code lock on it and Jacoby was taking the chance that his father hadn't changed the code yet. If he entered the right code, the alarm wouldn't go off. They might have a few extra minutes before anyone noticed them on the cameras. He just hoped they'd be able to get inside and subdue everyone before anyone got hurt.

After a quick glance at Den, Jacoby caught and held Kari's gaze for several long seconds. And when she smiled, he nodded and stepped up to the back door. Entering the code, he wasn't shocked when it worked. He was more shocked that an alarm didn't sound, and he didn't hear the crash of feet as guards came running.

Kyle slipped around him into the empty kitchen, followed by the wolves and Kaisie, Den close on their heels with Kari by his side.

No cook. Where the hell—

That's when Jacoby realized they'd stepped into a trap.

"Get out. No—"

Piercing pain slammed daggers into his head. It radiated outward, targeting every muscle in his body. He had no idea he could handle so much pain and still stay upright. Around him, everyone else seemed to be having the same reaction. They were all incapacitated.

And then his father stepped into the room.

"Hello, son. I had a feeling you'd be coming home. I'm sorry it had to end like this, but I'm sure you understand why you can't be allowed to have your sister. But we do thank you for delivering the goddess to us."

The tall, distinguished-looking man standing in the door to the kitchen had a smug smile on his sharp-boned face. Jacoby wanted to smack it off his face, but he was in too much pain to do much of anything. All he could do was watch as his father came closer. He didn't see the gun in his father's hand until he raised it and hit him with it.

Which was the stupidest thing that bastard could've done. The second the gun touched him, it brought him into complete focus. Vaguely he heard Kari scream but he couldn't afford to lose the connection to the metal. He had to trust Den to take care of her.

Even though the pain was intense, he managed to force himself to his feet, his grin making his father's brows rise in surprise.

"That's the last time you get to take a swing at me, Father. But thank you for proving that I'm doing the right thing."

———

KARI'S SCREAM cut off with a gasp as Jacoby stood and his father leveled the gun at his chest.

Jacoby said something that made his father sneer, but she had no idea what it was.

The pain spell being cast by one of the men in the room continued to scream in her ears, but she would take care of that. She was a healer. It was no match for her. Yes, it went against every molecule in her body. She'd been created to take away pain. With an effort, she moved Den, who'd covered her body with his much bigger one, trying to shield her. He fought her but, as she kept telling them, she was a goddess. And still a powerful one. She could take a little pain.

Forcing herself to hone in on the spell itself, she followed it back to the man standing behind Jacoby's father. He held no weapon but his lips moved silently, maintaining the casting. The spell required the caster to dig deep inside his psyche for the necessary fuel, which, in his case, was his childhood. A morass of misery and pain.

At any other time, she would've pitied him. Not today.

She took that pain, amplified it, and turned it back on him. It wasn't clean and it wasn't pretty. She saw the moment it hit him, saw the widening of his eyes and the dilation of his pupils, saw the hand he held out in front of him tremble then shake uncontrollably. In the next second, the spell stopped, and the wolves sprang into action, going after the men surrounding Jacoby's father.

But Kari only had eyes for Jacoby. He was facing off against his father across the room. She started for him, but Den grabbed her around the waist.

"No, he's got it. Let him handle this. We need to get Emelia. I promised him."

"I'm not leaving him alone with that man."

Den leaned in and spoke into her ear. "Trust him. He's got this. Help me get Emelia."

No. She couldn't do it. Jacoby needed her to stay. If anything happened to him and she wasn't here...

"Kari. *I* need your help. Jack doesn't."

Damn it. Damn, damn, damn. "Let's go."

She followed Den as he led her out of the room and away from the fighting, toward a staircase behind the kitchen. No one followed them, but Kari knew there had to be men guarding Emelia. Jacoby's father wouldn't allow her to be taken without a fight.

She hated to be right.

They hit the third floor at a run and nearly ran straight into the three guards in the hall.

Den didn't stop. He ran straight for them. They weren't expecting him, and their surprise gave him a few extra seconds to close the distance. The guards didn't notice her right away or thought she was no threat to them. Foolish mortals. Her power reached out and searched for their weaknesses, their fears, sought their most vulnerable points. Then she funneled all their worst fears back at them.

In the split second it took Den to reach them, their eyes widened, and they froze. Den took out two of them with solid right hooks to the jaw. Their eyes rolled back in their heads and they fell to the floor without raising a hand.

The last one, though... He fought back, as if her power had no effect on him. And maybe it didn't. Maybe he had a natural shield. Maybe he had strong magic himself.

It didn't matter. Den was on a mission and he wasn't about to be defeated. He took a few solid punches in the gut before he landed one on his opponent's chin. The guy's head jerked and he took a few unsteady steps backward but he didn't fall.

Den's lips curved in a hard smile before he took another swing. Relentless, Den followed with punch after punch, absorbing each of the man's slowly weakening blows while ramping up his own.

Finally the guy stumbled back against the wall and slumped to the ground, eyes closed.

Running to the door, she reached for it, but Den grabbed her hand a second before she made contact. Shaking his head silently, he grabbed it and gritted his teeth.

"Den! What's wrong?"

He didn't answer, just kept shaking his head though she could see he was in pain. Turning the knob made him grimace, but after a few long seconds, he shoved the door open and pushed through.

Almost immediately, he shuddered but didn't go down. He kept moving forward even though someone on the other side was throwing magic at him to slow him down. Every blow hit him like a fist, but as she came in behind him, he rushed the man in the middle of the room and took him to the ground.

The guy was smaller, almost slight, and he didn't have the muscle to go against Den. The *Mal* kept using his magic and Kari had to intervene. Focusing, she aimed directly at the young man, who cried out in pain the second she unleashed her power at him.

That sound physically hurt her, but she kept it up until she felt his power ebb away.

Finally, Den put the other man out with a crushing blow to the jaw that snapped his head back until it bounced off the floor and his eyes closed. Her immediate response was to heal him. She felt his pain, even though he was unconscious, but she also felt the other presence in the room. Looking around, she found the young woman cowering in a corner of the room. She sat on a bed, knees drawn up and her head bent. Kari couldn't see her face. But she felt the kinship, the knowledge that this girl was part of her.

It was hard to explain, and Kari wasn't sure the girl felt the same.

Kari's hands shook as she crossed the room. She wanted to stop to make sure Den was okay, but she could tell he was breathing and moving, so she figured he could wait a second for her to check on the girl.

"Emelia?"

Long black hair, exactly the shade of Jacoby's, streamed around her shoulders, looking like it hadn't seen a comb in days. Maybe longer. The white nightgown she wore had what looked like bloodstains around the hem.

Kari's anger began to boil until it threatened to spill over. If it did, she'd destroy every single *Mal* in the immediate vicinity. And when she said destroy, she meant kill. And that would make her lose a vital part of herself.

She took a deep breath. "Emelia, I'm not here to hurt you. I'm here to take you away. My name is Kari and I'm going to take you to your brother."

After a few seconds, the girl lifted her head. Kari was unprepared for the hatred focused on her.

"I know who you are. Stay away from me. I don't want your powers. I don't want anything to do with you. I just want you to leave me alone."

What the hell? Kari blinked at the girl, unsure what to do.

"I don't know what they told you, but I'm not here to make you do anything. I'm only here to free you. Don't you want to leave?"

Tears stained the girl's pretty face and her lips trembled, but her eyes shone with fear. Of Kari.

"I'm not going anywhere with you. If Jacoby's here, he can come get me himself. I'm not leaving until I see him."

Tinia's teat, what had they been telling this girl? Had they poisoned her mind against Kari?

"Emelia, that's enough." Den spoke from behind Kari, his voice strong, but Kari heard the breathless pain behind it. "We need to leave."

The girl blinked and focused her attention behind Kari. "Den? Is that you?"

"Yes, it is. I'm right here. Jacoby's downstairs. We need to leave."

"Father said you were working with them." The girl shook her head. "I didn't believe him."

"I'm not working with anyone but your brother. He's here to get you out."

"Then where is he?"

Kari's heart hurt at the confusion and pain in the girl's voice, but they were running out of time. Though she couldn't hear what was going on downstairs, she knew Jacoby couldn't hold out much longer on his own against his much stronger father.

They needed to get back downstairs. No more time for small talk.

"Your father was trying to kill him the last time we saw him." Kari deliberately hardened her tone. The girl needed to hear her and obey. Fast. "We need to get back downstairs and make sure that doesn't happen so we can leave. Every second we spend here is another second Jacoby has to face your father alone."

The girl looked at her again; this time her fear had receded slightly, and anger was starting to creep in. Good. She'd need that anger to get her out of here.

"I don't trust you."

"That's fine." Kari shrugged, trying not to feel offended. The girl didn't know her, and she'd been brainwashed by her father for most of her life. "I don't care. But you trust Den, right?"

The girl's mouth flattened into a line. Stubborn. Good. She'd need to hold on to that.

"Yes."

"Then listen to him. But if we wait any longer your brother is going to be injured."

Or could already be. And if that happened, Kari would make them all pay, most especially his father. Another two heartbeats passed before the girl slid to the side of the bed and stood. Her nightgown left her arms bare and Kari saw bruises on her biceps. As if someone had grabbed her and held her tightly.

You would think the girl would be willing to trust anyone who told her they were taking her away.

"I'll come. But you need to bring Tag. I'm not leaving without him." She pointed at the man on the floor. "I won't go without him."

Kari's eyes widened and her mouth dropped open. "You want to take your guard?"

Emelia looked her directly in the eyes. "He's not my guard. He's my protector."

"He's *Mal*." Den growled. "We're not taking him."

"Then I'm not leaving."

Kari was left speechless again, until she took a good look at the way the girl was staring at the man on the floor.

"Den."

His brows rose as he stood, shaking his head. "No way."

"Please."

The quiver in Emelia's voice must have reached Den because he sighed and stood. And even though he didn't look as strong as he normally did, he slung the other man over his shoulder.

"Let's get the hell out of here before he wakes up and tries to kill me again. *Vaffanculo*, your brother's going to kill me. And then he's gonna kill this guy. Fair warning, Eme."

"Thank you, Den." The girl turned back to Kari and fear showed in her eyes again, even though she didn't flinch as she curtsied. "Lady."

Kari wanted to sigh but she reined in the urge. They'd sort all of this out when they were all safely away from here. Which meant heading back downstairs and collecting the rest of their people.

Kari hoped like hell nothing had happened to Jacoby. If he'd been hurt...

All bets were off.

———

JACOBY SAW Kari and Den leave the room and breathed a silent sigh of relief, even though he hadn't completely neutralized his father yet. Jacoby's father was a powerful *Mal* and Jacoby had known he'd be a tough opponent.

He'd been betting on the fact that his father wouldn't kill him outright. That he'd have a few minutes, at least, before the man realized how much of a danger Jacoby was and decided he needed to die.

But that time was fast winding down.

His father's gaze narrowed as he stared at Jacoby, realization showing on his face. "You've gotten stronger. No, that's not right, is it? You've been strong, you've just been hiding it. Bravo, son. Too bad it won't do you any good now."

"You're not going to win this one." Jacoby knew the wolves were taking care of the other men behind him, but he also knew those men weren't the real threat. That was his father. "Surrender and we'll leave. You don't have to die."

"Oh, I don't plan on dying. And I think you're going to be disappointed if you think your sister's going to leave with you. She's not going to leave everything she knows to follow you. I'm her father. She'll do what I say. Especially when I control the man she loves."

Well, shit. He should've let the wolves deal with his father so he could get Emelia. "She won't stay. Not with you."

"Oh, but she definitely doesn't want to go with your little goddess. We've told Emelia exactly what's going to happen when the deities get their hands on her, how her life will never be her own again. We offered her freedom and the chance to rule. You offer her a life of servitude. Which one do you think she'll choose? She's no longer the foolish little girl who worshipped you."

"So you brainwashed her."

"No. We just told her what she needed to hear. It helps that most of it's true. The goddess isn't going to give up her mantle. Not without a fight. Emelia knows Akuhvitr will probably kill her."

"You don't know what you're talking about."

"I probably know more about it than you do. Your sister's seen what happens when someone tries to take the mantle. It's not pretty."

"Emelia's not stupid. She knows how much danger she's in with you. She'll leave."

"Then I guess I'll just have to take the option away from her."

His father pulled the trigger a split second before Jacoby realized he was going to do it. He wasn't taken off guard, but he was slow enough that the bullet got away from the gun before he could stop it.

Jacoby felt the punch as it hit him in the chest, felt the delayed burn even as he directed his power out and away from him. Surprise spread across his father's expression as the strength of Jacoby's spell hit him. He'd been practicing the spell for months, refining it, for this moment.

He used rage to fuel it, the rage he'd kept bottled for years. What had started as anger at his father for his neglect had become a honed blade. He had a single-minded purpose and that was to take his father out. No matter the cost.

Ignoring the pain from the bullet, he concentrated on the metal of the gun. Then he forced it to do what he wanted.

If you were watching closely, you'd think the gun was melting. It wasn't. It was deconstructing, becoming a liquid that seeped into his father's skin and into his blood.

His father's expression was puzzled at first, but not concerned. Until it hit his blood.

And then his expression changed. He grimaced at the first twinge of pain. His eyes narrowed and his mouth flattened. The hand he still held out in front of him shook and he looked at his arm as if it'd become alien, not something that was a part of him.

His mouth opened as if to scream but nothing emerged. Jacoby felt nothing as he watched his father contort as the burning metal spread, pumping through his body and arrowing straight to his heart.

"Jacoby."

He heard someone call his name, but he had to watch. He had to stand witness to what he'd done. What he'd become. Because this was who he was now.

A killer.

"Jacoby. We need to go."

Kari's voice. Calm, warm, steady. He heard no fear, no condemnation. Though he deserved it. Look what he'd done to his own father.

"Jacoby." Her voice was closer now and he felt her hand land on his arm, a comforting weight he didn't deserve. But he didn't pull away. "You're hurt. You need medical attention. Please, sweetheart. Come with me."

Hurt?

He looked down and saw the spreading bloodstain on his shirt.

And then the pain he'd been blocking hit him like a freight train. It took his breath away and left him gasping. And falling. But he never hit the floor.

Then everything went black.

TEN

"Are you sure he's going to be okay?"

Amity sighed but only said, "Yes, Kari, he's going to be fine," in exactly the same tone she'd used the five previous times she'd answered Kari's exact same question.

For the past ten hours, she'd been sitting by Jacoby's bedside in the *lucani* den, waiting for him to wake. She'd been so frightened he would die in her arms before they got him back to Amity. Kari had felt so useless, watching him go cold. And then suddenly Sal had appeared and transported them back to the den, where Amity had been waiting to heal him.

As much power as Kari retained, physical healing was Amity's specialty. Kari could heal the pain of a broken heart, but she couldn't fix that heart if it was nicked by a bullet.

Now, all she'd been able to do was wait for him to wake up.

And waiting sucked.

Especially when her replacement sat across the bed from her holding Jacoby's other hand.

Emelia seemed quiet, shy, reserved. Nothing at all like Kari. Which led to insanely stupid questions rolling through Kari's head.

Was this why she was being replaced? Because her people had decided she was worthless and didn't want her around anymore? Or had they simply forgotten her altogether and had decided on someone who was her polar opposite to be their new goddess?

And how absolutely ridiculous could you be?

Shaking her head, she looked up and caught Emelia staring at her. They hadn't said more than a few words to each other, but they'd been worried sick about Jacoby. Which was a total excuse that everyone had probably seen through. Kari was just a bitch and should own up to it. She wanted to stick her tongue out at herself.

You're a total bitch.

"Emelia, how are you holding up?"

The girl barely raised her head, her gaze brushing Kari's for a split second before lowering to stare at Jacoby's hand in hers.

"I'm fine, Lady Kari. Thank you for asking."

Oh yeah, this is going to go really well.

"I know this is strange but once Jacoby wakes up, we'll figure this out, okay?"

"Yes, Lady."

Now Kari wanted to bang her head against the wall. Luckily, Den walked into the room a second later. He'd been the one bright spot since they'd returned to the den. He'd barely left her side since he'd returned with Emelia. He'd held her hand or put his arm around her and drew her into his side. He'd been strong while she'd felt like she was coming apart at the seams. Maybe she was.

"Any change?"

His deep voice lit a fire inside her. Even though it was banked, it was still there. She just didn't feel complete. She wanted them both, wanted everything. And she had a feeling she wasn't going to have it.

Because Jacoby had been ready to give his life to save his sister. Kari wanted to weep at the selflessness of it, but she also wanted to curse and spit and hit him because he didn't want to fight to stay with her.

Which made her selfish, didn't it? Utterly and completely hopeless and unworthy.

And, oh yeah, a total melodrama queen.

Ugh.

After a deep sigh, she smiled up at Den, because she couldn't *not* smile at him.

"No. But Amity says he needs to sleep. That's how he'll heal."

"Then I guess I'm healed because I'm not asleep anymore."

"Jack!"

Emelia cried out and threw herself over her brother, hugging him tight as his arms went around her shoulders and brought her even closer. After he'd released the hand Kari had been holding.

"Eme. Thank the Gods. You're okay. Were you hurt?"

"No, I'm not. Den and Lady Kari made sure."

Kari drew away, though she couldn't go far because Den stood at her back, hands on her shoulders.

She wanted to be the one he embraced so tightly, be the first person he looked for when he woke.

But she knew how important Emelia was to him and she couldn't help but feel a little happy because he was so happy. She felt his joy at seeing his sister and her lips curved in a smile, which was what he saw when he glanced at her.

"Kari. Are you okay?"

"I'm fine. I'm so glad you're awake. I'm sure you'd like some time alone with your sister. I just wanted to make sure you were okay. I'm just going to...go find my sister."

"Kari—"

"Don't get up." She laid her hand on his shoulder and pushed him back into the bed. He went without a fight and she could tell he wasn't healed completely. Only rest would accomplish that. "You need to sleep. I'll be by to check on you later."

She could tell he wanted to say something more but then he glanced at his sister and he nodded.

"Thank you. Both of you."

He glanced at Den before looking back at Kari. She couldn't tell what he was thinking but it was probably better that way. She probably didn't want to know. She made her escape quickly because she felt tears hovering and she didn't want Jacoby to see them.

"Kari, are you okay?"

In the hall outside Jacoby's room in the *lucani* gathering hall, she forced a smile for Den. "I'm fine. I just need to...go."

His hand landed on her shoulder and stopped her in her tracks. "Kinda seems like you're running. And you know when you run, I have to follow."

This time she didn't have to force her smile. "I'm glad to hear that. I just need a few minutes to myself."

"Just make sure they're only a few minutes. I'm not leaving you. *We're* not leaving you. Even if you wanted us to go, I wouldn't. Not now. You know that, right?"

It sounded like a vow. One she wanted to believe. But things were different now. Jacoby had his sister and Den had his mother to think about.

And she was about to be completely obsolete.

She lifted her hand and stroked it down his cheek, loving the feel of his stubble against her palm. Even now wanting to feel it against her bare thighs.

"Thank you, Den. I just need a little time to...get some things in order."

His gaze narrowed but he nodded and didn't follow her when she walked away.

———

THREE DAYS LATER, Den had had enough.

Kari was avoiding him. Jacoby had healed completely but was withdrawn and preoccupied. Only his mom seemed to be on the mend and in good spirits.

She'd been meeting with the scientist who'd cured her son of the same disease killing Den's mom. She already looked a hundred percent better. He still had no idea what the *lucani* planned to do with them so that's where he was headed now. To talk to the *lucani* king.

He'd walked down the stairs to the office Cole kept in the community center, which was also where he and Jacoby continued to stay. It wasn't a prison but he knew if they'd wanted to go exploring, someone would've been on their asses immediately.

Knocking on the door, he wasn't surprised when Cole's personal guard, Dorian, opened it and waved him in.

The woman didn't say a lot and she didn't look at all threatening. But Den figured if she was guarding the king, she probably had a few tricks up her sleeve and he did not want to find out what those were.

"Den. Thanks for meeting with me. There are a few things we need to go over."

Cole didn't smile much, either, but Den didn't think that was because the guy didn't like him. He thought Cole was drowning in details. The guy obviously had a lot on his mind.

"No problem." He took the seat Cole waved at, even though he felt like he needed to stand at attention. He had a pretty good idea Cole got saluted on a regular basis but Den wasn't *lucani*.

He was Etruscan, however, and those ties ran deep. They worshipped the same gods and shared the same magic in their blood. Den just wasn't sure that was enough to earn him and Jacoby a place here.

"So." Cole leaned back in his chair, tapping the pen in his hand against the desktop. "Guess we should start with the obvious question first. Do you want to stay?"

Den's eyes widened as shock hit him. "I wasn't sure that was going to be an option."

"I wasn't either. But I've talked to Kari and I talked to your mom. Your mom's great, by the way. Glad to see she's doing better."

"Uh, thanks. I appreciate you letting Grace work with her."

Cole's lips twisted in a wry grin. "Yeah, I don't *let* Grace do anything. Grace does whatever the hell she wants and tells me to go to hell if I even attempt to tell her no."

Having met Grace Bellasario, Den understood Cole's amusement. The woman was a force of nature.

"So," Cole continued. "Are you planning to stay? Kari vouched for you but we're not the *Mal*. We don't conscript soldiers. If you want to stay, you pledge your loyalty and then you prove it. You don't..." He shrugged. "There are consequences."

Which Den figured included pain and death.

"I need to talk to Jacoby."

"So you two are a package deal?"

He thought for a few seconds before he answered that question. Then he nodded. "Yeah, we are."

Cole shrugged. "We can deal with that."

Then he stood and Den did, too, taking the hand Cole held across the desk. "Let me know by the end of the week."

Den nodded then headed for the door.

"Hey, Den?"

He turned, hand on the knob. "Yeah?"

"A little unsolicited advice?" Cole lifted an eyebrow and his grin now had a smart-ass curve to it. "When a goddess vouches for you, I'd make sure you properly thank her. They tend to get a little testy when they think you don't appreciate them."

He didn't bother to answer Cole, but he figured that didn't require a response.

What Cole didn't know was that he'd been trying to properly thank his goddess for the past three days but she'd been avoiding him like he had the plague.

She'd been to see Jacoby several times but he was being a dick. There was something up with him, and Den had yet to figure out what.

Of course, the guy's father had tried to kill him but Jacoby had killed him first. In a fairly horrific way with a power he barely knew how to control. That was sure to freak anyone out.

But Jacoby wouldn't talk. And his sister... *Vaffanculo*, she was downright silent compared to Jacoby. She'd refused to leave Jacoby's side, had requested they bring in a bed so she could sleep there as well. She had asked once about the man she'd insisted they bring with them but that had been it.

She was either terrified or plotting how to make them pay for stealing her away. And the few times he'd seen her in the same vicinity as Kari, she'd seemed to shrink into herself even more. And Kari had looked heartsick.

It was all a fucking mess.

And he felt like he was the only one who wanted to fix things.

Well, that was about to come to an end.

He didn't bother to knock on Jacoby's door when he got there; he just walked in. Emelia jumped and practically flattened herself against the wall to the left of the window, where she must've been standing, staring out like she did so much of the time.

Jacoby didn't look startled at all, sitting in front of the TV, probably because he knew the only person who'd come barging in here was Den.

"Hey, Eme, can you give us a few minutes?"

She blinked, as if she didn't understand the question. "Um, sure. Where should I go?"

"You know you're not a prisoner, right? Why don't you go downstairs? There's a common room with a library and a TV and some video games. And I think I saw a pinball machine."

She took a step toward the bed, looking at her brother as if she needed his permission. When he nodded, her shoulders slumped as she headed out the door.

As soon as the door closed behind her, Jacoby sighed. "We finally getting kicked out?"

"Why do you think that?"

"Why would they want to keep us around? We're a liability. The *Mal* are going to come after Eme, and I need to find somewhere we can hide. We need—"

"They offered to let us stay. They want us to stay."

Jacoby's jaw tensed before he shook his head. "Then they want to keep Eme, not us. They're just—"

"Did you not hear what I just said? They want us to stay. Cole said Kari vouched for us."

"She did?"

"Did you think she wouldn't?"

"What the hell was I supposed to think? I haven't seen her in days."

"Maybe because she figured you didn't want to see her. Christ, how dense can you be? You've been a fucking stone wall the past three days. You barely speak to anyone except Emelia. You haven't even talked to me. I figured you wanted to get the hell out of here and I was trying to decide how to get you to stay. I want to fucking stay. I want to stay with Kari. She needs us to watch her back, just like we need each other. But if you want to leave, then I'll follow. We stick together."

"How the hell do you even know she wants us to stay?"

There. That's what Den had been waiting to see. That spark of hope in Jacoby's eyes.

"Because she's been here the entire time. She hasn't left. She's waiting for us. We need to make sure she knows we need her as much as she needs us. She needs to know we're going to be here for her, that we're not going to take off and desert her."

"How the hell can you be sure?"

"Because I see the way she looks at you. And I know how I feel about her."

Jacoby fell silent, staring out the window again. "I'm not sure I'm fit to be around anyone, Den. This power... It's not like anything I've heard of before. I'm dangerous."

"So is she. Don't you get it? It doesn't matter. Your power is what's going to keep her safe. And I'll watch our backs. That's how this is gonna work. So get your head out of your ass and help me figure out how the fuck we're going to convince her she should give us another chance."

Jacoby's smile made a slow return.

"I'm in."

"KARI, I swear if you sigh one more time I'm going to throw my shoe at your damn head. Just get them together in one room and tell them they're being idiots and to stop screwing around. If you want them, tell them. Rom, back me up here."

"And that's our cue to leave." Rom shot out of the chair he'd been sitting in at the table in the cabin he and his cousin shared with Amity, grabbed Remy by the arm, and drew him to his feet as well. "Let's get the hell out of here before they start yelling and want us to take sides."

"Right behind you."

"No fair," Amity called out, though she was laughing as she did it. "Cowards!"

As they passed Amity, sitting in a chair close to the front door, they kissed her soundly before disappearing.

Kari couldn't blame them. She'd been miserable for the past three days. No wonder no one wanted to be around her.

So she sighed again and barely caught the pillow Amity threw at her. "Stop already. I get it, I get it. I'm an idiot."

"I didn't say that. But I will if it will make you stop moaning and do something."

"I honestly don't know what to do. I don't want them to think I'm pressuring them into staying. How will I be able to tell if they really want to stay or if they just feel they have to stay because I want them to and I'm a goddess?"

"How will you know if you don't ask?"

"I was waiting for them to say something."

"And if they don't?"

Her nose wrinkled and actual tears filled her eyes. Gah, how pathetic could she actually be?

Apparently, pretty damn pathetic.

It was Amity's turn to sigh. "Then you'll survive."

"Maybe..."

"Maybe what?" Amity's gaze narrowed. "Kari, what are you thinking?"

"Maybe they're not meant to be mine. Maybe...my time's passed."

Amity sat there silently for several seconds before she started to shake her head. "Were you knocked on the head recently? This isn't like you. You're not a quitter. You're the one who's always smiling. You're starting to worry me, Kari. And I don't like it?"

"Maybe I need to let them go. Maybe I don't—"

"Don't even go there." Amity had used her Goddess voice, the one that said she wasn't kidding around. Of course, Amity very rarely kidded.

Kari was the one who never took anything seriously. Maybe now that attitude was coming back to bite her in the ass.

Maybe Den and Jacoby would be better off without her. Who knew what they were going to do know that they were free of the *Mal*? It wasn't like they'd talked to her about it.

Hell, they'd barely talked to her at all.

"You need to snap out of this mood right now. And then you need to find a way to make those men want to stay. No one can resist you when you put your mind to something. You're a goddess. Remember that."

Kari smiled and nodded. "You're right. Of course, you're right."

She knew her sister didn't believe her, but it was all she could offer right now, and she left soon after that, wanting to be alone.

Which was also completely unlike her.

Walking back to the tiny cabin she'd taken on the outskirts of the *lucani* village, she tried not to feel sorry for herself. She hadn't wanted to leave the men alone at the den, but she hadn't wanted to crowd them, either. Guess that had been the wrong decision.

Apparently, she'd been making a lot of wrong decisions lately. But she honestly didn't know which decisions were the right ones any more.

Pushing open the door to her cabin, still wondering what her next step would be, she stepped inside—to find her men in the front room.

Den leaned against the front wall, where he must have been watching out the front window. Jacoby sat on the chair facing the door, gaze trained on her with laser precision.

She had to suppress a little squeal of joy, she was so happy to see them. But she bit her tongue and put all those happy thoughts on check for the moment. She still didn't know why they were here.

So instead of throwing herself at them, she kept her hands to herself. But she did do a thorough check of Jacoby with her powers. He seemed healed from the gunshot wound, body and mind. But his expression told her nothing about what she wanted to know. And her curiosity got the better of her.

"Are you here to tell me you're leaving?"

Ugh, how needy could she be? No wonder they'd been keeping their distance.

She wanted to take back the words as soon as they were out of her mouth. But it was honestly the only thing she wanted to know. The men exchanged a look before training their gazes on her again. And now, she felt a shimmer of heat spread through her.

"We're here to tell you we're *not* leaving." Jacoby rose to his feet and began to close the distance between them. "And to tell you we plan to stay as close to you as possible. Whether you want to admit it or not, you need us. You need us to watch your back. You get into way too much trouble on your own. We're going to make sure you have someone to pull you back when you need it."

"But we don't want to box you in." Den pushed away from the wall and stalked toward her, effectively boxing her between him and Jacoby.

Which was exactly where she wanted to be.

But it was almost too good to be true, to have them show up

here like this. Maybe she was dreaming. She reached out to touch them, both of them, and felt warm skin against her palms.

"But we need to know if this is what you want, Kari." Jacoby took another step closer. "You've got to say yes."

Her smile spread and she wanted to dance around the room in joy. Of course, that might send them running the other way. Then again, they hadn't run yet.

"If I say yes, will you shut up and kiss me?"

"Only if that yes means you realize this is a permanent situation." Jacoby put his hand over hers and brought her even closer, until she had to tip her head back to look him in the eyes.

Her lips curved in a smile that made heat flare in Jacoby's eyes, a heat that slid through her body faster than wildfire.

Den must have been able to read Jacoby's expression because he stepped up behind her and molded her body to his much larger one, his erection hot against her back.

Leaning down, he put his lips against her ear, making her shiver as he nipped at her lobe.

"Say the word, Kari."

Her breath hitched and her eyes closed as Jacoby leaned forward and pressed his lips to her neck.

"Yes."

ALSO BY STEPHANIE JULIAN

DARKLY ENCHANTED

Spell Bound

Moon Bound

REDTAILS HOCKEY

The Brick Wall

The Grinder

The Enforcer

The Instigator

The Playboy

The D-Man

The Machine

The Comeback Kid

FAST ICE

Bylines & Blue Lines

Hard Lines & Goal Lines

Deadlines & Red Lines

INDECENT

An Indecent Proposition

An Indecent Affair

An Indecent Arrangement

An Indecent Longing

An Indecent Desire

SALON GAMES

Invite Me In

Reserve My Nights

Expose My Desire

Keep My Secrets

Rock My Heart

LOVERS UNDERCOVER

Lovers & Lies

Sinners & Secrets

Beauty & Brains

Thieves & Thrills

ABOUT THE AUTHOR

Stephanie Julian is a USA Today and New York Times best-selling author of contemporary and paranormal romance. Make sure you sign up to receive all of her news at www.stephaniejulian.com

Published by Moonlit Night Publishing

Library of Congress Cataloging-in-Publication Data